# LOVING LYDIA

## MARYSE DAWSON

Published by Blushing Books
An Imprint of
ABCD Graphics and Design, Inc.
A Virginia Corporation
977 Seminole Trail #233
Charlottesville, VA 22901

Maryse Dawson
Loving Lydia

Print ISBN: 978-1-63954-115-7
v1

# CHAPTER 1

*WEST SUSSEX, THE YEAR OF OUR LORD 1671...*

*L*ydia Robins was cross. Decidedly so. Pursing her lips, she reached down for a pebble and threw it with all her might into the still waters of the lake. The loud impact startled one of the moorhens on the other side, and flapping its wings loudly, it quickly took cover amongst the rushes.

Lydia stared after it, wishing she could do the same. But no. That certainly wouldn't be allowed. She rolled her eyes and shook her head, causing her long blue-black hair to swish around her shoulders, the silky strands gleaming in the sunlight.

Why, oh why, did her mother always insist on inviting Cecily Walters to their soirées? Didn't she have enough acquaintances to choose from whom she could invite instead? Cecily was the most unreasonable person she knew and practically every time they met, they argued.

Her mother, of course, thought she was being difficult and that Cecily was merely a tad on the excitable side, declaring that Lydia should have more patience and try to curb her tongue a little. Lydia narrowed her eyes and, huffing under her breath, threw another pebble.

"I was going to say good morning but judging from your obvious vexation, I would say it is not. Am I correct?"

A deep voice broke into her thoughts and Lydia spun around to find Lord Hugh Danbye watching her, a hint of amusement in his dark brown eyes. He was their closest neighbour and had been a friend of the family for years. He was a handsome fellow, with shoulder length brown hair and a neat cavalier moustache. He held the title of Earl of Barnham and was considered quite the eligible bachelor. If he wasn't so much older and in possession of such a domineering persona, she might fancy herself in love with him. But he had told her off one too many times for her liking so even the notion of marriage to such a man was pushed swiftly aside.

At thirty-six, he wasn't exactly old, but in her opinion, a man nearer her own age would be far more suitable. And by suitable, she meant someone more accommodating and docile than the foreboding earl. Heaven knew what it would be like to have such an overbearing husband.

Unfortunately, thus far, no other suitor had even come close to his handsome good looks, and at the ripe old age of nineteen, life was beginning to pass her by.

She placed her hands on her hips and retorted angrily, "In answer to your question, Lord Danbye, no, it is most definitely not a good morning! Mama has invited Cecily Walters to tonight's soirée and you know that I detest her."

He shot her a look of commiseration. "Yes, she can be rather irksome but surely, you can avoid direct contact with her," he suggested. "Perhaps sit at the other end of the table and converse with others?"

"On this occasion, I cannot. There are to be only our two families present." She pulled a face. "Apparently, her mama has something important to tell us. I expect it is something trivial as usual but said in such a way that we should gasp with awe and pretend to be impressed." She flung her hand in the air dramatically, her eyes rolling with annoyance.

He chuckled. "Miss Robins, I am certain it will not be as bad as you portray it to be."

"Oh, I believe it will," Lydia muttered. She turned back to the lake and, concentrating hard, threw another pebble, wondering how the devil she was going to get through the evening with her faculties intact.

LORD DANBYE STUDIED Lydia's stiff little form as she took her frustration out on the pebbles she launched into the lake. She was a fiery little thing and possessed a wilful nature. One that he had, on occasion, had to curb by way of a verbal reprimand when her parents were not there to do so. But despite her precocious ways, she was a rare beauty. Her lustrous dark hair swept down her back, almost touching her pert little bottom and her striking blue eyes were enough to weaken the hardest of men. His thoughts took a deeper turn and he shifted uncomfortably as his manhood began to stir.

Clearing his throat, he said her name to gain her attention, "Miss Robins?"

She swung back around to face him, her brow lightly furrowed. "Hmmm?"

"The main reason I have come today is to tell you that I am returning to court for a few months. The king has requested a meeting with his officials."

She arched an enquiring eyebrow. "When do you leave?"

"In a few days. I have some affairs to get in order before I go."

"Do you know why the king wishes to see you?"

Lord Danbye stroked his moustache and for a moment his

face grew dark. "It would appear that the Dutch are being troublesome again."

"Oh. Think you there will be another war?"

"Mayhap. We shall see. But 'tis nothing for you to worry about. Will you walk with me to the house?" He held his arm out for her to take.

"Of course." She placed her small hand on his sleeve and they walked sedately back to the large house that Lydia had the good fortune to call home. Named Haven Manor, it had been built over two hundred years ago by one of her forebears and had been in her family ever since.

The gardens were equally as beautiful as the house, tended to by two gardeners, Tom and Rigby. It was May, and in her opinion, one of the most beautiful times of year. The trees were full, with new green growth and the early flowers were intoxicating with their heady scent. Lydia's father, Sir Ralph, was an amiable man but a stickler for having things done to his satisfaction—woe betide anyone who failed to do so, his gardeners included. So at any time of year, one could take a walk and not fail to admire the gardens' beauty.

Reaching the house, Lord Danbye stood to one side to allow Lydia to enter first. She did so with poise, and he found himself once again admiring her trim form as he followed her into the parlour.

Sir Ralph was reading the London Gazette and lowered it when he saw him. "Hugh, my boy. How lovely to see you. Take a seat."

He obliged by seating himself opposite. Lydia, he noted, opted to stand over by the window, distractedly winding one of her silky strands of hair through her slim fingers. She was so pretty but didn't seem to realise it. Another thing he found most appealing about her.

"Would you like something to drink, Hugh? A glass of port? A coffee?" Sir Ralph asked him.

"A glass of port would be splendid."

Sir Ralph beckoned his servant over with a crook of his finger and told him to pour the beverage for Lord Danbye.

"How goes the king?" Sir Ralph asked him.

"Very well, or at least he was the last time I saw him. I will be attending court at the end of the week, which leads me to why I am here. I wondered if you wished to accompany me? I know you have oft asked about Whitehall, and this would be a perfect opportunity for you to see for yourself."

"Nay, lad. I am much obliged that you thought of me but my foot is still giving me problems." He tapped his left leg with his walking stick. "Doctor says 'tis gout. All I can do is rest it. Bothersome, but there is little else I can do." He shrugged his shoulders. "'Tis not the first time I have had it and I doubt 'twill be the last."

"It must be painful," Lord Danbye commiserated.

"Yes, it is, but enough talk of this damned foot—how are things over at Seven Oaks?"

"Very well. I had a new wing built on the eastern side. You will have to come and visit when you are recovered. It looks rather splendid."

"I should like that. So will my wife. She is oft lamenting the fact that I do not go out enough, even though I tell her I am quite happy as I am," he added gruffly.

Lord Danbye chuckled. Lydia's mother was quite an assertive woman and as pleasant as she was, one could find her a little overbearing on occasion.

"Will you have a party to celebrate your new extension?" Lydia asked him, walking over, her eyes alight with interest. She perched her bottom on the arm of her father's chair. "It would be the perfect way to show it off?"

Lord Danbye raised an eyebrow. "I am not certain people would be that impressed."

"Of course, they would!" Lydia expressed, warming to her

theme. "Everyone loves a party and they will also get to view the new building. Yes, they will be impressed."

"I shall think on it. Parties take a lot of planning, and at the moment, my main concern is returning to court."

Just then the door opened and Hortense, Lydia's mother, breezed in. Lord Danbye immediately stood up, his good manners coming to the fore.

"Lord Danbye! How lovely to see you," she exclaimed, smiling broadly. "I have only just learned of your visit, otherwise I would have joined you sooner." She held out her hand for him to kiss, which he did with decorum.

"Lady Robins."

"You look decidedly well if I may say so," she noted, sweeping her gaze over him.

"Thank you. And may I return the compliment?"

She accepted his remark gracefully. "How kind of you to say so. I wonder, are you free this evening? We have guests coming and I would love you to join us."

"I have no prior engagements. I would be honoured."

He glanced at Lydia who smiled impishly and retorted, "How delightful. You can also endure Cecily Walters' unbearable company."

"Lydia!" her mother sharply reprimanded her.

Lydia rolled her eyes and walked over to the window, leaving Lord Danbye to make small talk with her mother and father. The dinner promised to be entertaining if nothing else.

THAT EVENING, dinner progressed surprisingly well. Cecily seemed slightly quieter than usual but it suited Lydia, for she had no desire to talk to her at all. She instead concentrated on conversing with Lord Danbye and her father.

At the end of the main course, Lydia's attention was

diverted by her mother asking, "Well, what is this news you wished to speak of, Lady Walters? I confess to be rather intrigued and simply cannot wait any longer to find out what it is."

Lady Walters dabbed the corners of her mouth delicately with her serviette and then her eyes sparkled with excitement as she said, "As you know, one of my dearest friends is the Duchess of Cleveland. She and I have been friends for many years now. Well, she has put in a good word or two and our fortunate daughters have been chosen to serve the queen. What do you say to that?" She sat back in her seat, a look of self-satisfaction on her face.

Lydia's jaw nearly dropped down onto the table. Serve the queen? Had she heard right?

Her mother was quick to reply. "It cannot be true? Surely?"

"Oh, it is, believe me." Lady Walters nodded her head emphatically. "They are expected at the end of this month. Is this news not exciting?"

"I confess, I had never envisaged Lydia going to court, but yes, 'tis most wondrous," Hortense replied.

Lydia raised her eyebrows, looking from one to the other before remarking, "Do I have a say in this?"

Lady Walters turned her head sharply and looked at her, aghast. "Surely, you have no objection?" The notion that anyone would reject such an offer was clearly unthinkable.

"Not as such," Lydia declared, "but it would have been nice to have been asked beforehand rather than just assuming I wish to go to Whitehall."

Lady Walters tutted loudly. "It is a great accolade not just for yourself, but for your family as well. Cecily has no such objection, do you, my darling?"

Cecily's eyes shone with excitement. "Not at all, Mama. I feel truly honoured to have been chosen to serve Queen Catherine." She quickly glanced at Lydia. "I confess, it will be a little

7

daunting at first, but you and I together can rely on one another to calm our nerves."

Lydia stared at her and raised an eyebrow. The last thing she wanted to do was rely on Cecily! But politeness meant she had to respond with something so she grudgingly offered, "I suppose."

～

THIS NEWS WASN'T WELCOMED by Lord Danbye, not at all. He had listened quietly to the interchange and felt compelled to speak out. "I do not wish to alarm you, but the king has a certain reputation," he interjected, trying to be as diplomatic as he could. "I am not certain it is a wise decision to send your daughters to court."

"All kings have a reputation, Hugh," countered Sir Ralph. "But both our daughters are virtuous and strong of mind. They would not be easily swayed."

"He is known to be very persuasive," Lord Danbye warned him, shooting Lydia a sideways glance.

"I think your worries are unfounded, Lord Danbye," stated Lady Walters. "I have no such fears. It will not only give them a step up in society but may even find them suitable husbands."

The thought of Lydia taking a husband sent a surge of jealousy through Lord Danbye so great that he wanted to slam his hand down on the table in anger. Instead, he had to make do with clenching his teeth. He had often fantasised about asking her to be his wife, but he was thirty-six, nearly double her age. Would she want a man so much older than herself? She had never shown any interest in him that way and he had had enough lovers to know the signs.

But the thought of her going to court filled him with dread. Lydia was young and, in his opinion, vulnerable, and to place her amongst the backbiting and often outwardly hostile members of the court was akin to throwing Daniel to the lions.

But her parents seemed not in the least worried. Perhaps they would be of a different opinion if they had seen and heard what he had when walking through the corridors and halls at Whitehall. The torrid whispers, the malicious gossip. At least he would be there to watch over her. It gave him some comfort at least.

The meal continued with the women chattering over what dresses to take and which items the girls should pack. Sir Ralph looked at Lord Danbye over their heads and with a wink of his eye and a nod of his head, the two men left the table and retired to the sanctity of the study.

THE NEXT DAY, Lord Danbye returned to Haven Manor. His intention, to forewarn Lydia of the iniquitous den she would soon find herself in. His previous night's sleep had been most troublesome and he had awoken with a pressing need to speak with her. Without her parents present, he hoped to be able to speak to her plainly. In his opinion, forewarned would hopefully be forearmed. Even better, perhaps he could persuade her not to go at all.

He found her wandering around the gardens, a small basket in one hand and a pair of scissors in the other. She wore a pale-yellow dress with a white lace collar and matching lace cuffs. Her hair was neatly pinned up today, the dark brown ringlets framing her petite face.

She looked up on hearing his approach and smiled. "Why, Lord Danbye, you are here again."

"Yes, I wondered if we may speak in private."

She looked at him astutely. "I assume you mean without my parents present."

He nodded and motioned to a nearby bench. She walked over and, placing her basket on the gravel path, sat down as he did the same.

"This is about me going to court, is it not?" she asked, raising an eyebrow. "I noted you had reservations yesterday."

"Yes, indeed I do." He rubbed his forehead, wondering how to phrase his words. "I know your parents are honoured that you have been chosen to attend the queen, but life there is far removed from the life you live down here in Sussex." He settled his eyes on her, his expression worried.

Lydia shrugged her slim shoulders. "I am no fool, Lord Danbye. If I hear any rumours or any whispers falling from licentious lips, then I will pay them no heed. I intend to do my duties as will be expected of me, but apart from that, I will keep myself to myself." She stood up and stared at him, laying a calming hand on his sleeve. She was so petite that their eyes were almost on a level. "You need not worry on my behalf."

"Life is not as simple as that, Miss Robins. If it were, I would have no cause for worry, but the court can be a dangerous place."

"I am fully aware that people can show you one face yet hide another. I will be perfectly fine. Truly."

"I am merely concerned."

"Well, you have no need to be," she admonished him. "Besides, surely we will encounter one another on occasion, and if I have any difficulties, I will be certain to seek you out."

"Very well. But promise me that if you experience any problems, even if they seem trivial, that you will tell me or your parents. I will come to you immediately," he declared sincerely.

"I believe you will and I thank you for it." She bent down and picked up her basket, placing the small woven receptacle over her arm. "Will you walk with me whilst I collect some more flowers?"

"Yes." He stood up and, keeping in pace with her small steps, followed her to a long line of rose bushes.

~

LYDIA WAS BEGINNING to get a little irritated with Lord Danbye's concern about her going to court. Good lord, he was acting more overprotective than her parents!

After her initial reluctance to go, mainly influenced by having to be in such close proximity with Cecily, she had decided that, in fact, it might be quite exciting. After all, she was nineteen now and certainly old enough to know her own mind and stand up for herself when the occasion arose. She was no lily-livered weakling and would have no hesitation in putting someone in their place if need be. A small frown marred her brow. Although that would obviously not apply to the king, but His Majesty was their sovereign, so surely, she could place her trust in him?

No, Lord Danbye was being overly cautious in her mind. She leaned forward to snip off a rose stem and rolled her eyes when he told her to be careful of the thorns.

Placing one hand on her hip while with the other, she brandished her scissors at him. "Lord Danbye, I have been cutting flowers for years. Do you think me addle-brained?"

She watched his handsome features change as her words sank home. His eyes darkened imperceptibly. "There is no need to be rude, Miss Robins." He went to cover her hand with his own. "Please, allow me to do it for you or perhaps one of the gardeners can assist you."

"No, there is no need." She pulled her hand back, putting the scissors out of his reach.

"Do you ever do as you are told?" he queried, giving her a stern look.

"Of course, I do, but not when the person asking is worrying needlessly," she huffed.

He raised an eyebrow. "Your reaction is exactly the reason I do not wish you to go to court. You are far too independent and headstrong." His mouth settled into a thin line of determination. "In fact, I am going to speak with your parents again right this minute."

Lydia gasped. "You cannot! I have already made up my mind to go and I will not have you impeding me." The devil in her quickly came to the fore and with a lightning-fast move, she reached up on tiptoe and promptly cut the feather off his hat. She watched with satisfaction as it floated down between them.

"You little madam!" Lord Danbye exclaimed, his eyes sparkling with anger. "I should spank you for that!"

Lydia's pretty mouth dropped open at his statement, her eyes wide. "You would never dare."

"Is that a challenge?"

"No, it most certainly is not." Lydia took a step backwards, realising that he was deadly serious. Her stomach roiled nervously. His expression was stern and Lydia realised she may have just made a critical error. She took another step back, her heart beginning to race. "It is only a feather. I merely played a little prank on you and I believe you are overreacting."

He folded his arms across his broad chest and looked at her astutely. "You see, this is the very reason I worry about you going to court. Your impudent nature will undoubtedly land you in trouble."

"Fie, not everyone will be as tiresome as you," she said rudely, glaring at him.

"You will apologise."

"No, I shall not!"

They stared at each other for a long moment, neither moving until Lord Danbye reached out to take her arm. It was Lydia's cue to skedaddle.

Dropping her basket and the offending scissors, she lifted up her skirts and ran for all she was worth. She could feel her heart hammering in her chest and her breathing become laboured as she tried to outrun him. But Lord Danbye was much quicker and she soon found herself captured. She struggled and kicked out, but his massive arms had her well and truly immobilised.

"Let me go! *Let me go!*" she shrieked, angry at having so easily been overpowered.

"No, my bad-tempered vixen. You are in need of a sound spanking and I intend to make sure you receive one," he said sternly.

"Unhand me!" she squealed, doing her utmost to break free of his vise-like grip.

Lord Danbye ignored her and she soon found herself upended over his knee, her bottom high up in the air. "This is undignified. You cannot treat me like this!" she objected through gritted teeth.

"You should have thought about that before acting like a child."

"'Tis not my fault if you cannot take a... *oh!*"

She gasped when she felt a rush of cold air on her buttocks, realising he had just exposed her bottom by throwing her skirts over her back.

"What are you doing? *Aooow!*"

She shrieked when his hand made contact with her bottom, leaving a painful sting. Before she had time to recover, it fell again, and again. She felt her body jolt forward with each spank and cried out indignantly, "Stop! It hurts! *Stop, I say!*"

He continued, despite her shrieks of outrage. It would seem he was hellbent on giving her a sound punishment regardless of anything she had to say. Her slim legs kicked uselessly into the air, her hands scrabbling around in front of her, trying to pull herself away from his punishing hand.

"You need a lesson in manners, Miss Robins. You seem to be under the illusion that there are no consequences for your naughty behaviour. I hope you will act with more decorum when you are at court."

Her bottom was on fire and each smack of his large, iron-like hand made her writhe in pain. There seemed to be no escape from the torturous onslaught. "You are mean, my lord. Please... *stop!*"

With a final swat to each buttock, he finally ceased, letting his hand lie still on her tender, heated flesh. She went to rise, but he kept her firmly pinned down. "An apology if you will?" he demanded, his deep voice filling the air.

Lydia huffed under her breath but had a feeling that if she failed to repent, then she would get more of the same. Reluctantly, she gave in. "I am sorry."

Finally, he allowed her to rise, which she did swiftly, hopping from foot to foot in front of him, whilst rubbing furiously at the backside. Her cheeks felt hot with embarrassment. God's bones —he had just seen her naked bottom! She let her skirts fall down into place and looked at him petulantly, her bottom lip thrust out in indignation.

Lord Danbye pointed his finger at her. "I hope you will learn from this. It is not how a lady behaves, do you understand?" he chided her.

She nodded sullenly.

"Now, I suggest you go inside and think upon your behaviour. When you attend court, I shall come to see you, to make sure all is well. Until then, my mischievous Miss Robins, I bid you adieu." He turned on his heel and made to leave.

"You are not going to dissuade my parents?" she asked him hesitantly.

He stopped mid-stride and looked at her over his shoulder. "Nay, Miss Robins. On reflection, I believe you have made up your mind to go, so I will not stop you. I simply take solace in the knowledge that I will be there to watch over you and keep you safe." He looked at her meaningfully before turning around and taking his leave.

Lydia watched him walk away, her bottom still smarting from his firm hand. He might warn her of the unscrupulous people at court, but the one she would have to truly watch out for was him. And it seemed he would be watching her very closely indeed.

Her mouth made a little moue and she placed a hand over her bottom protectively, wondering what she was truly letting herself in for.

# CHAPTER 2

*TWO WEEKS LATER...*

*L*ydia and Cecily arrived at court and after a briefing with Lady Castlemaine, who held the title the Duchess of Cleveland, they were promptly shown to their new quarters.

Unfortunately, Lydia was dismayed to find out that she would be sharing the room with Cecily, a fact that Cecily seemed to find wondrous. She had hoped to have her own room, but fate had deemed otherwise.

God's bones, it would mean no respite from Cecily's chattering. Plastering a smile on her face, Lydia decided to make the best of the situation. She had no other choice. Yet.

The room was more spacious than Lydia had presumed it would be. There were two separate beds, a small table and two chairs, and a small leaded window surrounded by thick plush curtains, overlooking a large courtyard. They also had a luxurious large woven rug between the beds.

Cecily threw herself down on one of the beds and bounced,

testing the comfort.

"'Tis most comfortable, Lydia. Do you want this one or the other for I have no preference."

"This one will suit me fine, Cecily." At the moment, she really didn't care which bed she had, as long as she had one, plus the fact she didn't have to share a bed with Cecily was a bonus. She wrinkled her nose at the thought of having to sleep next to her. At least things weren't that bad.

"When do we commence our duties?" Cecily continued. "I confess I hardly heard a word that the duchess said to us; my nerves got the better of me."

Lydia tutted. "You really must listen more, Cecily. She said that our duties will start tomorrow morning but we are to be introduced to Queen Catherine this evening. Now, I suggest we unpack our trunks and choose something suitable to wear." She looked down at her dusty travelling clothes. "These will most definitely need a clean."

"Are you nervous, Lydia?" Cecily asked, lying on her side and studying her.

"Of course, I am. It would be unnatural if I were not, but we shall put on a brave face else we will be eaten alive. Never show your weaknesses, Cecily, ever."

LATER THAT EVENING, the two girls were introduced to Queen Catherine of Braganza. Seated in her own suite of rooms, she sat upon a plush, upholstered chair and regarded the two girls solemnly. She was quite petite, with long dark brown hair swept up into fashionable ringlets. Of Portuguese origin, she had a honeyed complexion and sultry eyes.

The Duchess of Cleveland stood to their side and openly regarded the queen with a look of mild contempt.

Lydia noted it straight away but had no time to think on it before the queen addressed her. "Come forward, Miss Robins."

Her accent was relatively strong but her English was quite fluent. Lydia did as she was bid and approached silently before curtseying. "Your Majesty."

"You are very pretty."

Lydia felt a flush steal over her cheeks. "I thank you, Your Majesty."

"You will find me easy to serve as long as you remain both honest and trustworthy." She turned her gaze on Cecily. "Miss Walters, come hither."

Cecily did as she bid and curtseyed in front of her. Queen Catherine studied her just as closely, before remarking, "You resemble your mother very much. I have a great affection for Lady Walters. I hope you will honour her name by serving me well."

"Oh indeed, Your Majesty," Cecily gushed, her cheeks flushing with excitement.

"You will answer only to myself, the king, and Lady Castle-maine, no other. You will find that some of the palace residents may try to coerce you into deeds that need not concern you." She gave a little sigh. "People are not always as they seem, something I have had to find out for myself." Her eyes pointedly shot to Lady Castlemaine before returning to the girls. "My advice, my dear girls, is to keep yourself to yourself and ignore petty gossip, for there will be plenty."

She smiled serenely. "Now that we have been introduced, you may begin your duties. Go down to the kitchens together and fetch me a small platter of pastries. The cook knows what I like. Make haste!" She shooed them away with her hands and they quickly curtseyed before heading for the door. Once outside, they looked at each other, their eyes wide.

Lydia spoke first, her voice hushed. "Did you see the looks exchanged between the duchess and the queen?"

Cecily nodded. "There is animosity betwixt them, but why?"

"I know not, but we had better hurry up and organise the queen's pastries although I have no idea where the kitchens are." She looked along the corridor left and right, a small frown marring her brow.

She looked up and found one of the guards studying her, a hint of amusement on his face. She narrowed her eyes, a little vexed. "I presume you know where the kitchens are?" she asked him, knowing full well he had overheard their conversation.

"Yes, I was waiting for you to ask." He raised his hand and pointed down the corridor. "Turn right at the end, go down the stairs, turn left, go past the king's laboratory, continue past the Countess of Falmouth's rooms, then enter the great hall and simply follow your nose after that. There's always something cooking, you'll soon find it."

Lydia looked at him aghast, "We cannot remember all that!"

"You will. Although there are fifteen hundred rooms in the palace, so try not to get lost." He had the audacity to wink at her.

Lydia rolled her eyes and looked at Cecily just in time to see a sparkle of attraction in her eyes. Her cheeks were a soft shade of pink. Oh lord, she was blushing. If she was not mistaken, Cecily had taken a shine to the guard.

Grabbing her arm none too gently, Lydia began to usher her away and her voice laced with sarcasm, said to the guard, "Well, thank you so much for your detailed directions. I am certain we shall find it. You have been most kind."

Lydia quickly marched Cecily away before quietly chiding her, "Cecily, do not even think such thoughts!"

Cecily gasped and stopped dead in her tracks. "What do you mean?"

"I saw the way you looked at that guard," Lydia said pointedly.

Cecily went to say something else and then simply giggled. "There is nothing wrong in looking, Lydia."

"I thought so," Lydia noted smugly, "Well, ensure you keep it that way if you please. Your mother would be alarmed if she thought you were enamoured of a lowly guard."

"I am not enamoured of him. You are overreacting, Lydia." Cecily rolled her eyes. "God's bones."

"I am just warning you to be careful, 'tis all." They reached the winding stairwell and began their descent to the lower level. "He will bed you and cast you aside if he has his way," Lydia warned her. "Do not give him the opportunity."

"Not all men are so, Lydia. Besides, I would never fall for the charms of someone like him, even though he is one of the handsomest men I have ever set eyes upon."

They reached the bottom step and Lydia rounded on her. "You see! I knew you liked him."

Cecily giggled. "Admiring is one thing, acting upon it is another. Fear not, I intend to remain as chaste as when I arrived."

Lydia breathed a sigh of relief. "Thank the lord for that." She looked left and right up the long corridors. "By the rood, we will never find the kitchens."

Twenty minutes later, and with the help of several palace staff, they returned to the queen's rooms, anxious that they had taken too long but satisfied they had completed their first task.

The queen smiled at them when they put the tray down and told them to take a seat. "Now you have accomplished your first duty, I will expect you to be much quicker next time. You will soon find your way around—Whitehall is a large palace but very beautiful. You will enjoy your time here." She stood up and walked over to one of the leaded windows, her voluminous skirts swishing with each step. "Do you enjoy masked balls?"

Lydia was the first to respond. "I have never attended one, Your Majesty, but I have heard they are most lavish."

"They are indeed. The king is holding one tomorrow night and I wish both of you to be present at my side."

Lydia gulped. "Truly?"

"Yes, and I shall have a mask made for both of you. I presume you have brought suitable dresses with you?"

Cecily began to talk about the dresses she had brought with her and as Lydia listened to her incessant chatter, she wondered how the queen could stand her endless babbling, but it didn't seem to bother her.

Lydia sat quietly eating a delicious pastry the queen had offered her and wondered if they would get to meet the king in person. The thought was an intimidating one but quite exciting at the same time.

THE NEXT EVENING, Lydia and Cecily walked behind Queen Catherine and Lady Castlemaine as they approached the large hall where the ball was being held. The music had reached their ears well before they arrived at the open door and Lydia's heart was already fluttering with apprehension. Would they be welcomed or shunned as newcomers? Would anyone even notice two new ladies-in-waiting?

King Charles was already present and the dancing well underway when they stepped inside the lavish hall. Lydia looked around, her eyes wide with wonder. There were so many people and their costumes were so vibrant and colourful. Masks adorned nearly every face, golds and reds, greens and blues—it was something Lydia had never experienced before and she drank it all in with wonder. Her parents had held balls but they were tiny in comparison to this lavish event. It was a sight to behold.

The guests parted for them as soon as they beheld their queen and the music stopped immediately. Queen Catherine approached her husband, elegance and poise in every step. He stood up from his throne and walked down the small steps to greet her, a broad smile on his face.

"Queen Catherine." His deep voice seemed to fill the room, commanding but at the same time respectful.

"Your Majesty." She curtseyed and looked to the floor. Lady Castlemaine, however, curtseyed but held his gaze, her eyes full of seduction. Charles' gaze rested on her briefly before leading the queen up to the throne.

Lydia and Cecily stood behind Lady Castlemaine, quietly wondering where they were supposed to go. Lydia was thankful she had her mask on because her cheeks were sure to be as red as a beetroot. So many people were staring at them that it was a little disconcerting. She had never felt comfortable being the centre of attention and it seemed they were just that at the moment.

She was relieved when Lady Castlemaine turned around and instructed them to follow her, which they did without question. With so many eyes on them, it was unsettling to say the least. She took them to the side of the room and, raising her hand dismissively, disappeared into the crowd without a by your leave. Lydia stared after her, wondering what both she and Cecily were supposed to do. The queen had mentioned to them that she wanted them by her side, but at the moment her whole attention was on her husband and it would seem their services were not required.

The king raised his hand to the musicians and when the music started up again, the dancing resumed.

Lydia glanced at Cecily and saw her face reflected how she felt too.

"What do we do, Lydia?" Cecily asked nervously, her voice just loud enough to carry over the sound of the music. "Are we allowed to dance?"

"I think so. I mean, I assume so. The queen told us as much, did she not?"

"But do we need her permission?"

Lydia shrugged. "I know not. It seems as though she has left us to our own devices and has settled her attention on the king. I think a little dancing will be fine. She will soon bellow if it is not." She grinned, and Cecily giggled in response.

"Yes she is not shy in coming forward."

Just then a serving girl walked past, carrying a tray of drinks so Lydia reached out and took two. She handed one to Cecily, saying, "A little courage methinks."

"Yes!"

Lydia sniffed the drink before taking a big gulp and then nearly choked on it. It was much stronger than she was used to and as it hit the back of her throat, it made her cough. She suddenly felt a hand patting her on the back.

"Better?" a deep voice drawled.

Even with his mask on, she knew it was Lord Danbye. She blinked her tear-filled eyes and smiled beneath her mask. "Lord Danbye. I think you just saved me." Her voice sounded raspy.

He laughed, a deep rumble in his chest. "Yes, the punch is a little heady—I suggest the wine next time. Would you like me to get one for you now?" he offered.

"If you please."

He took the glass from her hands and looked at Cecily. "And for you, Miss Walters?"

Cecily shook her head. "No, thank you. This is just fine."

"You are certain?" He raised his eyebrows, seemingly surprised that she was enjoying the strong drink.

Cecily giggled and took another sip. "It is quite delicious."

"Very well."

Lydia watched Lord Danbye disappear as he went in search of a more palatable drink. He stood out amongst the other guests because of his height and broad shoulders and she found herself naturally admiring his physique, then immediately admonished herself. Hadn't their last encounter involved him spanking her bottom? Her lips thinned when she remembered the hot feeling in her backside. Mayhap she shouldn't even be talking to him.

Cecily interrupted her thoughts by laying a hand on her sleeve. "This gentleman has asked me to dance. Will you be all right on your own?"

Lydia had been so deep in thought that she hadn't noticed the man approach Cecily. He bowed politely when she noticed him and she nodded her head in return. "Of course. I will be fine. Go and have fun, Cecily. I will wait for Lord Danbye to return."

Cecily placed her drink on the table and happily allowed her new acquaintance to lead her off for her first dance of the night. Lydia couldn't help but smile at her obvious happiness. She only hoped her partner would feel the same once he'd listened to her endless babble.

Lord Danbye returned in moments and handed her a small glass of wine which she accepted gracefully. She took a hesitant sip and was delighted to find it far more palatable than her previous drink.

"It is more to your liking?" Lord Danbye enquired.

"Yes, it is much more pleasant." She lowered the glass and, her eyes sparkling with slight indignation, commented, "I had not thought to see you so soon, my lord. Especially after our last encounter."

She wasn't certain whether she should forgive him or not, although his thoughtfulness over the punch was rather gallant. He looked very smart, adorned in a dark blue long coat, grey waistcoat and black britches, his long hair reaching below his shoulders. He had no need of a powdered wig which many of the others, including the king, chose to wear.

"You mean when I had to chastise you?" he said, his eyes fastening on hers.

She shifted uncomfortably and, raising her small chin defiantly, muttered, "If that is the way you wish to remember it, then yes."

He chuckled, seemingly amused at her response. "You would do well to remember that only naughty girls get spanked."

"I am not naughty, I was merely having a little fun—"

"At my expense," he interrupted her. "Sometimes, my dear Miss Robins, you have to learn that there is a time and a place for everything and a way to behave."

His eyes bored into hers and she had the sense to look away. She was still unrepentant and given the chance, she would do it again. Only this time, she would run a bit faster! But best he didn't know that.

She took another sip of wine and decided to change the subject. "Do you like these functions, Lord Danbye?"

"I confess I rarely attend these balls, but when I knew the queen would be attending, I decided to come. Where the queen goes, so do her ladies-in-waiting."

"So you wished to check up on me?" she queried.

"In a word, yes," he answered simply. "How do you find it so far?"

Lydia studied him. He did seem sincere and genuinely concerned to know how she fared. She shrugged her slender shoulders. "This is only my second day, but I find the queen to be extremely pleasant."

"And how do you find the Duchess of Cleveland?" he asked in a low voice.

Lydia looked at him sharply and whispered, "Do you dislike her?"

"I find her rather arrogant and she trifles in affairs that should not concern her. She did have the king's ear, but not so much now that Louise de Keroualle is in his favour."

"Who is she?"

Lord Danbye looked around the room until his eyes fell on a

brunette on the other side of the room. "See the woman standing over there wearing the red and silver mask. That is her."

"When you say she has the king's favour, do you mean that he and she…"

"Yes, that is exactly so."

Lydia's eyes widened. "But he is a married man."

Lord Danbye emitted a low, mirthless laugh. "You have a lot to learn about the king, little one. He is a man with a vigorous appetite. It is exactly what I tried to tell your parents, but they failed to listen. Be wary of him, Miss Robins."

"Indeed, I shall." She took another sip of wine. "But I am certain he will have no interest in someone like me."

"A pretty face is all it takes. Now, may I have the honour of this dance?"

"You wish to dance with me?"

"Yes."

She chewed her bottom lip, deciding whether she should or not. Hesitantly, she asked, "The queen will not be cross that Cecily and I are dancing, will she?"

"Of course not," he replied. "You attend the queen when she summons you, but during a ball, you are allowed some freedom." He glanced over to the dance area. "You see, Lady Castlemaine is indulging herself."

Lydia followed his gaze to see Lady Castlemaine dancing very demurely with a man wearing a jewel studded mask.

Lord Danbye held out his hand and she placed her small one in his. He led her over to the dance area and they began to dance. The music was lively and Lydia soon lost herself in the heady atmosphere. She hadn't envisaged court life being so much fun. It was quite exhilarating and far removed from her home life.

"Does this occur often, my lord?" she asked.

"Yes. Both the king and queen enjoy festivities. You will find life at court far from dull."

"I think I am going to like it here." She grinned.

"Remember what I told you before—do not hesitate to ask for me should you come across any problems."

"Where shall I find you? Have you taken lodgings nearby?"

"No, I reside here at court."

"Oh, you have your own rooms here?" Lydia said, impressed.

"Yes, some of our meetings with the king can last hours, days even, and it is easier for me to stay here, rather than find lodgings elsewhere. Many of the nobles have their own rooms within the palace."

"It is a splendid idea." Knowing he was so close was a comforting thought. As long as he didn't spank her for anything he deemed unsuitable behaviour, then all would be well.

The dance ended and Lord Danbye went to escort her off the dance floor but was stopped when the king approached them. Lord Danbye immediately bowed and Lydia curtseyed.

"The queen informs me you are one of her new maids of honour?" the king said, looking Lydia up and down.

"Yes, Your Majesty."

"Will you favour me with a dance?"

"Of course." Her hands trembled as he took them in his own and led her back onto the dance floor. Lord Danbye politely stepped aside and watched them from the side lines.

The music started and the king began to lead Lydia around the dance floor. "You tremble? Am I that intimidating?" he said softly. He lifted his mask, revealing a rather handsome visage. "Is that better?" His eyes crinkled at the corners and Lydia responded with a soft giggle.

"There, you see, that's better. I scare you no longer." He smiled. "Now come, lift your mask so I may see you properly."

Slightly breathless, Lydia lifted her mask slowly and looked up at him. His eyes darkened ever so slightly. "Beautiful. Quite beautiful."

Lydia swallowed hard, not knowing quite how to respond

and quickly replaced her mask, finding comfort behind the disguise.

The king stepped in time with the music, drawing her close and then back again. "What is your name?" he asked.

"Lydia Robins, Your Majesty."

"And how old are you, Lydia Robins?"

"Nineteen, Your Majesty."

"You look younger than nineteen, but then you are an innocent compared to the ladies of the court. I find you very refreshing."

He spun her around and his eyes piercing hers, he asked, "Would you like to join me tomorrow? I have several horses racing and I think you would enjoy it. The atmosphere can be quite merry, I assure you."

Lydia's heart skipped a beat. Why was he showing interest in her? "I know not, Your Majesty. I am uncertain as to whether the queen would allow me to come."

"Of course, she will. I shall tell her myself."

She had no idea how to say no or even if she could say no. So she kept quiet. The queen would soon tell her if she thought it acceptable for her to go or not.

The dance ended and the king inclined his head. "Until tomorrow, Lydia Robins."

She curtseyed. "Your Majesty."

He walked off and Lydia quickly walked over to the side. Lord Danbye was waiting for her, his face full of concern.

"It would seem you have caught the king's eye earlier than I would have thought. What did he say to you?"

"He asked me if I wanted to join him tomorrow; he will be racing some horses and told me that I would find it entertaining."

"Indeed you will, but tread carefully, Miss Robins, for not only have you caught the king's attention but I fear his current mistress has now noticed you."

Lydia turned around and found Louise de Keroualle staring at her from across the hall. Even from this distance, she could see her eyes glittering with hatred through the slits in her mask. God's bones, had she made an enemy already?

～

THE NEXT MORNING was taken up with the daily routine of catering to the queen's needs. She took her breakfast in bed and after having her hair neatly fashioned by Lady Castlemaine, she waved her hand in the general direction of the door and demanded, "Miss Walters, Miss Robins, bring me my britches, the burgundy ones."

Lydia paused on the way to the door. Had she heard right? "My pardon, Your Majesty, but did you say britches?"

Queen Catherine regarded her with amusement. "Indeed, I did. Do not seem shocked; for why should I not? Why should britches be solely worn by men?"

Lydia thought about it for a second and then replied, "I know not—it is just I have never seen a woman wear them before."

"This will be a new experience for you then. Make haste, the pair of you."

Lydia followed Cecily out of the room and they walked along the corridor to the rooms containing the queen's wardrobe. It was vast and it took them a little while to locate the correct garments.

Lydia held up the ensemble and pulled a face. "How free thinking our queen is! I do not think I would dare wear such clothing. Can you imagine what our parents would say?"

Cecily exhaled slowly, her eyes wide as she regarded the garment before her. "My mama would faint."

Gathering the clothing, they walked back up the corridor. Just as they reached the door to the queen's rooms, the guards changed shift and Lydia saw with dismay that one of them was the guard Cecily had taken a shine to. He gave Cecily a wink as she walked past him and Lydia tutted loudly to show her disapproval, shooting him a look of disdain.

Once inside, she hissed to Cecily to ignore him, but she knew it fell on deaf ears just by looking at her face. She was totally enamoured of him, but she had no time to dwell on it for the queen was beckoning them over.

They soon had Queen Catherine dressed and she stood before them, her hands on her hips, proudly showing off her manly attire. "There, you see. I am quite respectable. Now I am going outside to play with my dogs. You will join me and see for yourself just how easily one can manoeuvre in such wonderful garments."

"Your Majesty, if you have no further need of me, I must attend my children," Lady Castlemaine interjected regally.

The queen dismissed her with a wave of her hand and sailed out of the room, Lydia and Cecily following quickly behind. It would seem she had little time for Lady Castlemaine and personally, Lydia couldn't blame her. The woman had six children by the king and poor Queen Catherine had none.

It made Lydia admire her even more than she already did. She was not so certain that she could be so tolerant under the same circumstances.

Pushing thoughts of Lady Castlemaine aside, Lydia followed the queen outside onto the palace grounds where, as promised, she showed them exactly how agile one could be wearing a man's attire. The sight was something Lydia would never forget.

# CHAPTER 3

After lunch and with the queen's knowledge, Lydia found herself seated next to the king outside in the park next to the palace. She presumed there to be about thirty people present and ten or so guards.

The weather was perfect, a warm spring day with just a light breeze. Lydia's pale blue gown and fair complexion caught the attention of several of the king's guests. They cast curious glances her way but seemed far more interested in the horses than in her—something she was thankful for.

Several horses were lined up opposite them and getting ready to race, their riders doing their best to control the feisty animals. The queen had chosen not to be present but had quite happily given permission for Lydia to attend.

"Which one shall I bet on, Lydia Robins?" King Charles asked her. "Whom do you favour?"

Lydia chewed her bottom lip and studied the horses. "I like the black one with the thick mane."

"Very well. I will wager coin on it and if it wins, you shall have the money."

"Oh, Your Majesty. I could not accept that," she objected.

"Of course, you can. I have said so!" He turned to the jockeys. "On my mark." He raised his handkerchief and, waiting a couple of seconds, brought it sweeping down. The horses were off.

The small crowd cheered loudly, urging their favourite horse to reach the finishing line first. It was all very exciting and Lydia sat on the edge of her seat as her horse raced towards the ribbon at the end of the course.

She almost forgot she was in the presence of the king, for when her chosen horse broke through the ribbon in first place, she couldn't resist the urge to celebrate and jumped up from her seat, clapping loudly.

"Well done, my lady! You have a keen eye for a good horse," King Charles remarked, his eyes twinkling with merriment at her obvious joy.

"I do not know about that. I just liked the look of him, Your Majesty. I am certainly no expert." Lydia grinned.

"Well, my lady, let us see if your luck continues. Pick another winner for this next race."

Lydia had a very enjoyable afternoon and returned to her rooms rather richer than she had left. She stowed the coins away carefully, hiding the little purse in one of her shoes. Lady Castlemaine had warned them to keep valuables safely hidden. Even with their rooms locked, one could never be too careful.

Just as she placed her shoe back in the cupboard, there was a knock on the door. She walked over to open it, but the handle was already turning and the door was quickly thrust open. Lydia was a little disconcerted to see it was Louise de Keroualle. She strode straight in without asking, her chin in the air, an imperious look on her face.

Lydia stared at her in annoyance and although she was wary of her, she couldn't help remark, "Madame, should you not wait for permission to enter someone's private quarters?"

Louise ignored her comment, and her eyes narrowed, she said, "I will come straight to the point. The king is mine. If you think to steal him from me, then you are mistaken." Her voice was clipped with a strong French accent.

Her words took Lydia aback and she immediately retorted, "I have no interest in the king, other than to serve him and the queen to my best ability. I do not want him in the way you speak of, I assure you."

Louise emitted a humourless laugh. "Ha! You mean to play the virgin and entice him into your bed, but it will not work."

"I am not playing a virgin, madame," Lydia protested. "I *am* a virgin and I certainly do not seek to bed with the king!"

"I do not believe you," she snarled back. "Why would you not wish the accolade of sleeping with our king? All women do. But I will not have it, do you hear? You think you will gain power in the household by becoming his mistress, but you will not. I will see that you do not!"

She said it with such venom that for a moment, Lydia was speechless. Finding her voice, she replied, "I would not sacrifice my honour for power. I will marry one day and I intend to be a virgin when I do. You have my word upon that."

Louise snorted in disbelief. "Your word? I have seen the way you look at Charles and I like it not. Just be warned that should you dare to bed him, your life here will become unbearable."

Lydia's temper began to rise. How dare she just barge her way into her chamber and accuse her thusly. "You are wasting your breath. I have no interest in the king, other than to serve him."

"We shall see. Just know that I will be watching you and so will many others."

Before Lydia could say anything else, she swept out of the room as quickly as she had entered, the smell of her perfume left lingering in the air, her brunette ringlets almost bouncing, such was her indignation.

Lydia sat down on the bed with a thump, her heart pounding in her chest and her hands shaking. What an odious woman and such blatant unwarranted jealousy. What on earth did the king see in her? He had surely never seen this side of her, for he would cast her aside. No man would put up with such behaviour. God's bones!

Lydia shook her head with dismay. Well, now it was confirmed, she had indeed made an enemy, even if it was through no fault of her own.

LATER THAT NIGHT, when the queen had retired for the evening and she no longer required her services, Lydia went in search of Lord Danbye. He had told her to call upon him in times of difficulty and she dearly needed to talk to him about the confrontation with Louise de Keroualle.

Her visit, although unprovoked, had unsettled her and she needed to confide in someone. She had told Cecily what had happened but she wanted to talk to someone more experienced and more to the point, someone she could trust.

After asking the guards along the way, she finally located Lord Danbye's rooms. They were not far from the king's suite of rooms. Taking a deep breath, she knocked on the door and waited for a response.

It didn't take long. She heard footsteps and then the door opened a few inches, revealing Lord Danbye in a state of undress. His chest was bare and he sported only a pair of loose britches.

Lydia's eyes widened a fraction and she spun around, presenting her back to him, but not before she had taken in an eyeful of his rippling muscles and lean torso.

"Forgive me, Lord Danbye!" she said, a little shocked.

"Miss Robins! It is rather late to be knocking upon my door. Are you in trouble?"

"Not exactly, but I must speak with you and it is the only opportunity I have had to do so."

"Can it not wait until tomorrow?"

She shook her head. "I would rather talk about it now. I do not mean to inconvenience you but—"

He interrupted her softly, "No, no. It is no inconvenience to me. It is just that you have caught me unawares. Forgive my state of undress." She heard the door creak as he opened it wider, and turning back around, she entered his rooms.

"Take a seat and I will make myself presentable. I had just retired for the night."

She chewed on her bottom lip, unable to stop her eyes feasting on his perfectly honed body. He was magnificent. She felt heat steal over her cheeks and quickly looked down at the floor. What must he think of her, staring at him like that?

LORD DANBYE COULDN'T HELP but notice how her eyes assessed him, but far from finding it impolite, it heartened him. For why would a maiden stare at him so if she had no interest in him? With a perk to his step, he entered his bedroom and picked up a ruffled shirt from the chair, quickly donning it to cover his bare chest.

Striding back into his main room, he found her staring out his windows. He had views overlooking the privy gardens, and even though the sun had set a while ago, one could still see the pristinely kept gardens from the last vestiges of light falling upon them.

"Is all well, Miss Robins?" he asked.

She spun around and he saw her eyes were troubled. Taking one of her hands, he led her over to a seat and motioned for her to sit down.

"What has happened?" he asked.

"Louise de Keroualle paid me a visit."

"Oh? From your tone, I would gather it was not a pleasant one?"

Lydia shook her head. "No, She accused me of wishing to become the king's mistress!"

"Good lord. The king only has to glance in another woman's direction and Louise thinks he is smitten." He paused a moment before adding, "Although, in some cases, that has been known to happen." He looked back at Lydia. "He did make a point of singling you out at the ball. How was he at the races? Did he pay you any special attention?"

Lydia worried her bottom lip. "I cannot say he paid me any more attention than the other women present. At least, not that I noticed."

Lord Danbye walked over to a cabinet and poured them both a small glass of wine. Handing her one, he advised, "Do not let him turn your head, Miss Robins. He would never force you but he can be very persuasive, promising you gifts and anything your heart desires. Do not be swayed by his promises."

He watched Lydia's eyes darken with anger and she swiftly retorted, "I have quite a strong will, Lord Danbye!"

"Yes, you can be a little rebel on occasion, but this is the king we are talking of."

"I do not care who he is! I would tell him to shove his promises somewhere I would not rather say!"

Lord Danbye's eyes widened. "By the rood, Miss Robins, you would be wise to keep such wild ideas to yourself. If anyone overheard such remarks, you could find yourself in a lot of trouble."

Lydia snorted. "I care not!"

"You will care if your glib remarks reach the king's ears, believe me." He placed his glass down and walked over to her. "I will have your promise that you will never utter those words, ever."

She looked up at him with a disgruntled expression. "If I am not put in that position, then I will never have to utter them."

"Miss Robins, your promise?" he demanded sternly. "Or do you need another spanking?"

She rolled her eyes and reluctantly bit out, "Very well, I promise not to say them again. I just hope the occasion never arises in the first place."

"As do I," he agreed. "Now, I suggest you go back to your room and get some sleep. I will be vigilant and listen to any rumours that Louise de Keroualle may have an issue with you, but remember, come to me if you need me."

She stood up and handed him the empty glass, covering her mouth and yawning at the same time. "Goodness, I am tired. I bid you goodnight, Lord Danbye and thank you."

He walked to the door and opened it for her. The temptation to kiss her almost overwhelmed him but he managed to control it. "Go quickly now and be strong."

She smiled and left his room. Closing the door behind her, he thought about his words. Was she strong enough to withstand the king's advances should he wish to pursue her? He was handsome, rich and courteous. It would take someone very strong indeed to deny him.

THE NEXT FEW days passed quietly and Lydia began to think that Louise de Keroualle had totally overreacted over the king having an interest in her. Since the day at the races, he had not made any move to seek her out which Lydia was extremely thankful about.

Queen Catherine was proving to be a pleasure to serve. She had a quick wit and although she had a fiery temper on her when the occasion warranted it, she treated them with respect, something Lydia was a little surprised about.

The interaction between her and Lady Castlemaine was quite entertaining. Lady Castlemaine could sometimes be quite scathing but the queen always had a quick retort, leaving Lady Castlemaine gulping air like a fish out of water. It was hard to stifle her mirth sometimes, but when Lady Castlemaine fixed her with a warning look, she soon quietened. She would not like to get on the wrong side of that woman. She was most intimidating.

One morning, just as she was putting some of the queen's clothing away with Cecily in the wardrobe room, Lady Castlemaine joined them.

"Cecily, would you fetch the queen her mid-morning refreshments?" she instructed her. "I will finish the clothing." Her voice brooked no argument.

Cecily smiled." Of course."

When she had gone, Lady Castlemaine fixed her gaze on Lydia. "I see the king has taken a fancy to you," she said matter of factly.

Lydia couldn't help but roll her eyes a little. "Not you as well!"

"Oh? Someone else has noticed?" she queried, her eyes alight with interest.

Lydia nodded her head. "Yes, Louise de Keroualle."

"Oh, did she now? That is interesting," she said slowly.

Lydia saw a calculating look enter Lady Castlemaine's eyes and was immediately on her guard. "Why is it interesting?" she queried.

"It means she is jealous, my dear. Did she say something to you?"

"Yes, she was most annoyed and accused me of trying to gain the king's favour. She seems to think that I am interested in bedding him when I have no intention of doing so at all. I am here to serve the queen and that is all I intend to do."

"So she has her nose put out of joint." Lady Castlemaine

tapped her lip with her finger slowly, her eyes sparkling with almost, one could say, amusement.

"It would seem so and it is all unfounded. I cannot help it if the king looks at me. Mayhap he does find me desirous but it is certainly not reciprocated, I assure you."

Lady Castlemaine laid a calming hand on her sleeve. "Do not fret, my dear. Ignore Louise de Keroualle. She is a conniving, selfish woman who seeks to keep the king for herself. If he knew her true nature, then I am certain he would cast her aside, but at the moment he is a little blinded by lust."

"Even if he does cast her aside, I do not wish to fill that void," Lydia expressed, shaking her head.

"Even if that means gaining power and riches?" Lady Castlemaine queried softly.

"I care not for power or riches. I am quite content as I am. I would certainly never sacrifice my honour for such things."

"You would also have influence beyond your wildest dreams so never say never, my dear. One day you may need to rely on your most treasured possession—your innocence."

Lydia shut the drawer with a little more force than intended and said, "I hope that day never comes, Lady Castlemaine. Now if you will excuse me, I shall return to the queen's chambers."

Her skirts swished as she swept out of the room, her small heels echoing a clipped staccato along the corridor showing her indignance. Why wouldn't people leave her alone?

Her mouth thinned with determination. Well, she wasn't going to let it stop her enjoying her time at court. She would take each day as it came and deal with whatever came her way. A vision of Lord Danbye entered her mind and her mouth lifted up in a smile, her eyes softening. At least she had the handsome Lord Danbye to rely on. Her thoughts turned from his face to his muscled torso and a feeling of desire ripped through her, so strong that she stopped in her tracks.

She caught her bottom lip with her teeth uneasily. Was she falling in love with Lord Danbye? Could it be?

LADY CASTLEMAINE WATCHED HER LEAVE, noting her elegant poise. She was a beautiful girl and although she couldn't help but feel jealous that the king's attention had fallen on her, she did think it could be beneficial to usurping the odious Louise de Keroualle from her current position as the king's favourite. In doing so, perhaps he would lavish attention on her once more.

She would encourage Lydia Robins to be seen by the king as often as possible and make sure she was at her prettiest. When he fell for her charms, which it seemed he was already well on his way to doing, she would intervene before the king could act on his desires and somehow have Lydia removed from court.

She smiled wickedly. Yes, Louise de Keroualle would soon find herself pushed aside for another and maybe she would then see how it felt to be so discarded.

THAT NIGHT, Lydia confided in Cecily. They were lying in their separate beds, facing each other, the candle on the small table between them. She had found that spending time with Cecily wasn't as bad as she had thought it would be. Yes, she was most talkative, but at court, it didn't seem to bother her so much. Perhaps because it took the onus off her and gave her time to observe rather than participate.

"My goodness, Lydia," Cecily said. "I declare those two women are as conniving as each other."

"My thoughts exactly. I did not come here to catch the king's eye. My job is to serve the queen and that is all I intend to do."

For a moment, Cecily's eyes grew dreamy. "He is very handsome, though, Lydia."

"So? Just because someone is handsome does not mean I am going to let him, well, let him... do *that!*" She plumped her pillow up angrily. "I intend to make a suitable marriage one day and I wish to wed my husband as virginal as I am now."

"What will you do if the king commands it, though?" Cecily wondered. "What would he do if you said no?"

"I care not what he thinks!" Lydia said heatedly, "If he truly cares about his subjects, then he will be more chivalrous than that. If not, I will flee back home without a backward glance, and fie on him if he wishes to pursue me."

"Those are very brave words, Lydia, but on a serious note, I do not think you have to worry too much. From all accounts, I have heard he possesses a kind nature so I cannot see he would force you to bed him."

"I hope you are right," Lydia worried.

"John seems to think so."

Lydia sat bolt upright and looked at Cecily sharply. "John?" Even in the dim, flickering candlelight, she could see Cecily's face blush. "Oh lord, you mean the guard! Have you been talking to him?"

Cecily sat up as well and raised her chin slightly. "His name is John Russell and before you say anything, there is nothing wrong in talking to one of the guards!"

"Not unless he has taken a liking to you, which we both know to be true."

"So what if he likes me? It does not stop me from talking to him."

Lydia sighed heavily. "Well, all I can say to you is be careful, Cecily. Keep him at arm's length and do not let his words charm you. Just imagine what your mother would say if she thought there was something between you?"

"You will not tell her, will you?" Cecily asked, her eyes wide.

"No but if it is as innocent as you say, then there is nothing to tell, is there?" Lydia crooked an eyebrow, looking at her suspiciously.

"Indeed, there is not."

"Good, then let us get some sleep, else we will never be able to get up on time in the morning."

She leaned over and blew the candle out, leaving them both in darkness. Her head filled with thoughts of repelling any advances by the king, and Cecily's, quite the opposite when she thought of John, the most handsome man she had ever laid eyes upon.

# CHAPTER 4

*T*he days at court continued to be pleasant, not in the least because Lady Castlemaine was absent. Why she wasn't in attendance, Lydia knew not and cared even less. She just knew a great sense of relief and realised how intimidating the woman could be.

The queen was fond of being outdoors and, at this moment, watching her play with her dogs outside, dressed in her manly britches, was quite entertaining. The king didn't seem to mind her wearing such attire and Lydia very much doubted Queen Catherine would give a hoot if he did. She was petite but very strong minded. She smiled, realising she could almost be describing herself.

She had seen little of Lord Danbye, but it was comforting to know that he was at court if she needed him. She thought back to the last time she had called upon him in his rooms and felt her cheeks grow warm. Lord, he had a magnificent body. He also had a quiet strength about him that made her feel safe and secure. A frown marred her brow. If only he didn't feel the need to spank her, then he would make a most suitable husband.

She had seen a few men about the court who had piqued her

interest but none as handsome or commanding as Lord Danbye. But there was plenty of time for finding a suitable husband. For now, she had queenly duties to see to.

The queen was beckoning her over, so she quickly joined her. "Your Majesty?"

"Lydia, please take Rulf over to the guard. He is becoming a little over excited. I will ask Haversham to give him some more training, as he is becoming too much of a handful. Cecily and I will take the other two dogs over to the far side of the park."

Lydia eyed Rulf, the Irish Wolfhound who stared back at her, his tail wagging and his tongue hanging loosely out as he panted. Even though he wasn't fully grown, he was almost as big as she was. Placing her hand beneath his leather collar, she began to pull him towards the palace, but Rulf had other ideas. Focussing his attention on the queen and Cecily whilst they led the other two dogs away, Rulf tried to follow them.

"Come on, Rulf, do not be difficult," Lydia said through gritted teeth, pulling on his collar with all her might. He barked in response and then, without warning, took off towards the other dogs. Lydia immediately lost her balance and fell face first onto the lawn. She raised her face, coughing and spitting out bits of dust and grass.

Suddenly, she felt a hand under her elbow, assisting her to rise. "My lady, I admit it is considered mannerly to curtsey to your king, but I think you have taken it too far."

It was King Charles and he was laughing at her misfortune but his voice was full of good humour. He helped her to her feet and she wiped her mouth and face, blushing profusely.

"Your Majesty. Forgive me, but the dog caught me unawares."

"Yes, I saw it all. Damned animal should be whipped."

"Heavens! You would not do such a thing?" she said, aghast.

He smiled and shook his head. "No! Of course not. I merely jest. They are the queen's dogs and it is up to her how she trains them." He frowned and looked in their direction. "I fear she is not doing a very good job so far."

He looked back to Lydia, his eyes crinkling with mirth. "Lydia Robins. What am I going to do with you?"

Lydia gulped. "I know not, Your Majesty."

"Come with me. I think I have the very thing."

"Oh, I... um..."

"Fear not, my manservant will tell the queen where you are." He turned and raised a finger in the air. Instantly, a servant came running over. "Inform the queen that Miss Robins will be with me this afternoon."

The servant glanced at her, a hint of curiosity in his eyes, and then headed off towards the queen as instructed.

The king held his arm out for Lydia to take. She placed her arm through his and laid her hand flat on his sleeve. Good lord, if tongues weren't wagging already, they would be on fire by now. By the rood, this was all she needed.

"You find court life enjoyable, Miss Robins?" the king asked her.

"Indeed, Your Majesty. Although I find it a little intimidating at times." She was referring to Lady Castlemaine and Louise but she certainly wouldn't reveal that.

"People can be, shall we say, conniving when they want to be," he noted. "Stick by your friends and do not listen to court gossip. Do you have friends here?"

"Yes, Cecily Walters and Lord Danbye."

"Oh, yes, Lord Danbye. A fine fellow and very trustworthy. He is not one to beat about the bush, something I like very much about him, and therefore I consider him a friend. I depend on my friends to deal with me honestly." He stopped walking and looked down at her, his hand covering her own. "Can I count you amongst them?"

Lydia blushed profusely, his look was so intense. "Of course, Your Majesty."

"And I hope I can trust you to speak the truth when I ask."

Lydia nodded, not quite sure where this was going.

"Ah, here we are," the king said. A servant opened the doors for them and they entered into the palace. He led her down several corridors until they reached his apartments. Ushering her inside, he took her into a lavish room filled with sumptuous looking chairs, a big ornate carpet and several paintings on the wall.

"Take a seat. I won't be a moment." He disappeared through a small door to one side.

Lydia tentatively sank down into one of the chairs and looked around. Everything was so extravagant but at the same time, so beautiful. She looked at the paintings, each one as intricate as the next. One caught her eye and she stared at it, noting the resemblance to the king.

"My father," the king said, returning.

"Pardon, Your Majesty?"

"The painting you are looking at—it is of my father."

"Oh! I was just thinking you looked like him."

"He was a handsome man and his life ended far too soon." He stood for a moment, staring at the painting, his face pensive.

Lydia felt a pang of sympathy and her heart softened. "I am sorry, Your Majesty."

He shrugged. "As am I, but I have had plenty of time for regrets although I grieve for him still, in quiet moments. But we will not dwell on past times, Lydia Robins. Sit back and let me wipe those stains from your pretty face."

Lydia suddenly noticed what he had in his hands, a small bowl of water and some squares of cloth. Her eyes widened. "Your Majesty, you cannot do such a thing. It is not seemly! That is not a king's duty!"

He chuckled and knelt down in front of her. "That is for me to decide. Now, close your eyes."

Realising she had little choice, she did as he bid and gently lowered her lashes. She felt the cloth touch her face and tried to stay still whilst he cleansed the dust from her face, dipping the cloth in the water several times.

"There, you are clean again."

She opened her eyes and was a little disconcerted to find him only inches away. His eyes were a deep brown and he held her gaze unashamedly.

Lydia moistened her lips and noticed that his eyes quickly followed the movement of her tongue.

Swallowing hard, she went to rise but he placed his hand on her shoulder. "Do you like it here, Miss Robins?"

"Y-yes, everyone is most courteous." she said hesitantly.

He gave a wry smile. "Even Lady Castlemaine?"

"Well…"

"You know she is not your friend?" he said, standing up.

"I would not consider her a friend, but she has been quite kind."

He raised an eyebrow. "Her kindness is not without calculation, I assure you."

It sounded as though the king had little respect for Lady Castlemaine yet she had been told by some of the other ladies-in-waiting that she was still his lover. Perhaps he was tiring of her. After all, he had also taken Louise de Keroualle to his bed. The thought made her brow furrow.

"Do not let it bother you, Miss Robins. Just be aware." He walked over to an ornate table and reached for a decanter of wine. "Now, you shall take a glass of wine with me and tell me all about yourself. I have a hankering to know more about you."

Lydia accepted the glass and as the wine flowed, she became more relaxed in his company, her tongue loosening as the alcohol slipped through her slender body.

Charles proved to be a very intelligent man and extremely witty, recalling humorous anecdotes throughout their conversation.

By the time Lydia had consumed two glasses of wine, she felt quite lightheaded. "Goodness, Your Majesty, I will be unable to serve the queen this evening if I take another glass."

"Then I shall not offer it," he quipped. "I do not fancy being on the sharp end of the queen's tongue."

Lydia giggled and hiccoughed at the same time, her eyes growing wide with embarrassment. "Oh! Forgive me, Your Majesty!" She placed a hand over her mouth.

He laughed and slapped his thigh. "I find you quite delightful, Miss Robins." He studied her for a long moment before saying, "I would have you do something for me, if you will, Miss Robins. I find you to be of an honest character, which is the only reason I ask."

"Oh?"

"I fear Lady Castlemaine has taken another lover and I wish to find out who it is. She has had many but this one eludes me. I want you to gain her confidence if you can and inform me of your findings. Intercept any letters she sends, even if they seem innocent. I would know their content."

Lydia quickly began to sober up rapidly. "Why me, Your Majesty?"

"As I said, I find you to be trustworthy. It is a rare thing at court."

"But what if she finds out my intentions?"

"It is of no consequence, she can do you no harm. But I would advise that you do everything in your means to make sure she doesn't find out. It would be in both our interests."

"Very well," Lydia agreed slowly, her mind whirring. "How should I contact you if I am privy to such information?"

"You can approach me anytime but please use caution and you are not to tell anyone of our conversation. No one!"

His face grew serious and Lydia gulped nervously, quickly replying. "Of course."

She left the king's rooms feeling a little intimidated. What a task he had set her! Lady Castlemaine was a force to be reckoned with and if she had an inkling of what had passed between her and the king, then she knew who would come the worse off and it wasn't going to be the king.

~

OVER THE NEXT FEW DAYS, Lydia engaged Lady Castlemaine in conversation as often as she could, asking her advice on anything and everything without seeming too obvious. It seemed to work wonders and it wasn't long before an opportunity arose that Lydia had not expected to happen quite so soon.

"Lydia, would you be a dear and deliver a small note for me?" Lady Castlemaine approached her whilst she was clearing the queen's supper tray.

"Certainly."

"Leave that, I shall see to it." Lady Castlemaine stared at her hard. "You must give this to John Churchill, no other, do you understand?"

"Of course. Where shall I find him?"

"He has a room by the wood yard. The guards will direct you if needed." She glanced over to the queen, who was already in bed and talking to Cecily. "Go now. The queen will not miss you." She reached into her skirts and drew out a small, folded note. "Conceal this upon your person and make haste. Try to be as inconspicuous as possible."

Lydia took the note, quickly slipped it into her bodice and left the queen's rooms. However, instead of looking for the wood yard, she made straight for her own room. Unlocking the door, she slipped inside and rushed over to the table. Withdrawing the note, she turned it over. It was sealed with wax but to her relief, it was plain and bore no identifying signet ring indentation. She would easily be able to seal it again without anyone's knowledge.

Taking a seat, she quickly broke the seal and began to read, her eyes widening as the contents were revealed to her. Good lord, Lady Castlemaine was rather descriptive with her words! Some of them made her blush, they were so intimate. It would seem that John Churchill was the very man the king was wondering about.

She put the note down and thought hard. If she failed to deliver the note, then Lady Castlemaine would wonder what she had done with it and might even find out about her duplicity, but if she told the king, then what proof did she have? An idea sprang to mind. Perhaps if she copied the letter then she could not only give a copy to the king and he could read for himself what the note contained but she could deliver the original to John Churchill, and neither he nor Lady Castlemaine would suspect a thing.

Opening the small drawer beneath the table, she took out a small piece of paper and dipping her quill in the ink pot on the desk, she began to copy the note, word for word.

Lydia found the wood yard with relative ease and slipped the note beneath John Churchill's door. She had no wish to see him face to face, certainly not after reading the contents of the letter.

The copied note was safe in her bodice. Now all she had to do was get it to the king. Retracing her steps, she headed back towards the main palace. She was so deep in thought that she failed to notice Lord Danbye approaching.

"Miss Robins."

His voice startled her and she emitted a shocked gasp. "Lord Danbye!"

He immediately noticed something amiss. "Is something wrong?"

"No, no, not at all." She gulped. She could feel her cheeks

blushing, and stammered, "I-I was just on my way back to my room."

He looked over her shoulder and then fixed his eyes on her. "Where have you been?"

Lady Castlemaine had told her to be discreet so taking a deep breath, she answered glibly, "Oh, nowhere in particular, just having an evening walk, taking in the air."

He looked at her for a long moment and she maintained his gaze, trying her best to look innocent. What if he had seen her put the note beneath John Churchill's door? God's bones! He would wish for an explanation, of that there was no doubt.

"I will walk with you," he stated.

"Oh, you do not have to do that."

"I wish to. I have not seen you for a few days. You can tell me how you fare."

Realising he wasn't going to take no for an answer, she decided she had no choice than to allow him to accompany her back to her room without raising suspicion. So smiling brightly, she slipped her arm through his and they made their way back along the many corridors. They reached her room and she showed him inside. He was so tall, he made the room look tiny.

"Please take a seat, Lord Danbye. Would you care for a drink? I have some wine."

"Not at the moment, thank you." He was looking at her suspiciously and it was making her feel extremely unsettled. She twiddled nervously with a lock of her hair.

"Have you become enamoured of someone, Miss Robins?"

Lydia felt her cheeks grow warm and shook her head. "Most certainly not! What has led you to suppose such a thing?"

"The note you pushed beneath a certain scoundrel's door."

By the rood, he had seen her. She immediately went on the defensive. "You are mistaken."

She watched him shake his head slowly, his eyes watching her like a hawk. "No, I saw you do it and now, the fact that you are trying to deceive me, affirms my belief that you are doing something untoward."

Lydia's eyes flashed with anger. "I am doing no such thing. Besides, if I was, what business is it of yours?"

His jaw tightened. "Desist with this attitude, Miss Robins, it does not become you."

"I do not have attitude!" She balled her fists by her side, angry at being interrogated. "I think you should leave."

"No, not until you tell me what is going on."

She shook her head. "You are prying into matters that do not concern you."

He stood up and walked over to her. Placing his hand on her chin, he made her look up at him. "I promised your parents that I would keep you safe and I intend to do just that, so you will explain to me, right this minute, what business you have with John Churchill or I will make you tell me."

Lydia's stomach did a nervous flip. "If you think you are going to spank me, then you can think again!"

"If you do not tell me, I *will* spank you. Make no bones about it, Miss Robins."

His eyes were dark with anger, his jaw set tight, and it should have warned Lydia to comply but her stubborn nature made her refuse to reveal anything to him. He was being far too over-bearing and she would tell him so. "Fie! You can threaten me all you like but I will tell you nothing!"

Muttering an oath, he placed a firm hand on her arm and dragged her over to the bed. She tried to dig her feet in and struggled like fury, but it had no effect and she soon found herself face down over his lap, her skirts thrown over her back and a stinging slap landing firmly on her bottom.

She shrieked loudly and kicked her legs but Lord Danbye ignored her, pinning her firmly against his waist. "You are far too wilful," he admonished her.

He brought his hand swinging down and delivered several

well-aimed swats to her rounded bottom. Lydia protested loudly, but he ignored her complaints, intent on administering a sound spanking for her bad attitude.

"Ouch! Aow!" she wailed. "That hurts!"

"Good, I hope it does," he admonished sternly.

He gave her another five sharp smacks, and then laying his palm over one buttock as a warning, he asked her again, "Tell me what business you have with John Churchill or I will continue spanking you until you do."

Lydia's bottom was smarting like fury and she knew he meant what he said. But the king had warned her to tell no one of her mission. But she would have to tell him something, else he carry on with spanking her. Reluctantly, she told him that the letter was from Lady Castlemaine to John and she was just the messenger. Which was the truth, or at least, partly the truth.

Lord Danbye immediately released his tight grip and let her go. She jumped up, wasting not a moment to rub her poor bruised posterior better whilst shooting him a look of discontent.

"Why did you not say so?" Lord Danbye reprimanded her. "If you think to protect Lady Castlemaine, then you have no idea what type of woman you are dealing with."

"Why are you so high-handed with me?" Lydia demanded, her bottom lip thrust out with vexation.

"Because I care about you. John Churchill is a young knave and you are far too good for him. He would treat you abysmally. Now I know that it is, in fact, Lady Castlemaine who amuses him, then I am relieved. It would suit you well to tell the truth in the future." His eyes lowered as he noticed something on the floor. "You have dropped something."

Lydia looked down and her eyes widened in alarm. It was the copy of Lady Castlemaine's letter. It must have dropped out of her bodice when he had thrown her across his lap. She bent down and snatched it up, her heart racing nervously. Her bottom was sore enough and if he found out she hadn't been entirely honest with him, then he could add several more swats. She was certain of it.

"Oh, yes. That is a note for Cecily." She quickly walked over to the small bureau and, opening the drawer, shoved the letter inside. She hardly dared look at Lord Danbye for fear he would ask about the contents but thankfully, although his gaze was a little dubious, he refrained from asking.

He stood up and walked over to her, taking her small hand in one of his. "I suggest that you refrain from delivering any further notes on behalf of Lady Castlemaine. That woman is dangerous and I think you need to stay out of trouble, Miss Robins."

"I never intend to get into trouble," she explained, her mouth making a little moue.

"Maybe not, but curiously, trouble seems to follow you around." He lifted her hand and kissed her knuckles. The feeling was exquisite and set Lydia's heart racing, this time not from fear, but desire.

She felt her cheeks grow hot as his deep eyes looked into hers. "Goodnight, Miss Robins."

When he had left, she sat back down on the bed, mindful of her sore bottom, and rubbed the back of her hand where his firm lips had touched her skin. His dominance, although annoying, somehow stirred something in her, a deep admiration. He was so strong and virile, no dandy like some of the men she had seen at court. No, the more she saw of other men, the more she admired Lord Danbye. If she could learn to behave, then perhaps marriage to him would be just what she needed. But the question was, could she?

# CHAPTER 5

*T*he king stroked his hand down Louise de Keroualle's curves and she purred suggestively. "I have missed you in my bed these past few days, Your Majesty."

He chuckled. "Am I to believe you took no others in your bed during my absence?"

He had been away at one of his hunting lodges for several days and had only just returned. She looked at him askance. "Of course, I have not!"

He continued to stroke her skin, running his hand up over her hip and laying his palm against one voluptuous breast. He cupped it, squeezing gently. "'Tis not what the rumours suggest."

She slapped his hand away and sat up, annoyed. "And do you always believe rumours?"

"There is no need to take umbrage, my sweet Louise. I listen to the rumours but I do not always believe them. Besides, if it were true, it does not cause me undue concern, for I also seek my pleasures elsewhere on occasion."

She settled back down, her tousled hair falling in abundance around her shoulders. Laying a hand on his chest, she said, "Talking of pleasures, Your Majesty, I have noted the way you look at Miss Robins, and it displeases me. Surely, you have no need to look elsewhere—do I not give you enough pleasure?" She circled a finger on his chest.

He kissed her softly parted lips. "You are in my heart, Louise, but do not presume to tell me how to live my life." She went to speak further and he kissed her soundly, leaving her in no doubt that the conversation was now closed.

LYDIA HAD BEEN at court for nearly a month and was discovering that intrigue and lies were commonplace amongst the many residents. From the wealthy noble to the lowly chambermaid, everyone seemed to have an agenda.

It was all very tiring, and most nights Lydia went to sleep as soon as her head hit the pillow. As much as she found the balls, the gaming and the horse racing exciting, not to mention numerous other activities, she sometimes yearned for her quiet life at home in Barnham.

She had delivered her copied note to the king the morning after her stand-off with Lord Danbye. Having the letter in her room had felt akin to having a loaded cannon. The sooner she had rid herself of it, the better.

She had managed to catch the king's eye as he walked in the gardens and within minutes had given him the note, which he quickly concealed upon his person. He had told her to bring him more if she acquired them and reiterated how important it was to keep her mission secret.

She truly wished he had never chosen her to become his spy. How long he wished her to continue, she knew not. Just thinking about it, gave her a headache. She tucked an errant strand of hair behind her ear, pushed the worrisome thoughts aside and concentrated on her morning's task of sifting through the queen's linen. Cecily was beside her, humming happily.

"You seem very happy this morning, Cecily," she noted.

"Yes, the sun is out, the sky is blue and I am enjoying my work. What more reason to be happy?" she gushed.

Lifting up a pillow sham to the light to look for any marks, Lydia commented knowingly, "You have been seeing John Russell again, have you not?" She put the fabric down and placed her hands on her hips. "Do not even think of denying it."

"I was not about to," declared Cecily. "I am having fun, and without Mama and Papa here, watching over my every move, I can allow myself a little freedom."

Lydia tutted loudly, "And what if someone sees you two together? What will happen then?"

"Oh fie, we are extremely discreet. No one will find out."

"You seem very confident," she exclaimed before querying, "do you truly love him?"

Cecily cocked her head and twisted her mouth as she pondered Lydia's demand before replying, "Perhaps it is love, I cannot say." She shrugged her shoulders and giggled. "But a little flirtation does no harm."

"Does he see it that way? As harmless fun?"

"I think he understands that is all it can be. My parents would never allow us to marry so whilst I am here and do not have the duties of a wife, I aim to amuse myself."

"Have you kissed him?"

Cecily giggled. "Often."

Lydia's eyes widened. "When do you find the time? I have not seen you with him."

"Of course, you have not. We are both very careful. I slip out of our room when you are asleep but never stay out too long. Just enough to have a little fun."

"Have a care, Cecily. If anyone were to discover you two together, you could be instantly dismissed and so would he."

"You worry too much, Lydia. Do not fret about us, truly."

Their conversation was interrupted by a messenger. "Miss Robins? His Majesty requests that you attend him directly."

"Oh. He wishes to see my right now?" Lydia asked.

The messenger nodded. "If you would follow me?"

Lydia glanced at Cecily. Her eyes were wide with surprise, so Lydia just shrugged her slender shoulders in response and quickly followed the messenger. What did the king want to see her for? Was it something to do with Lady Castlemaine?

Nervously, she followed the messenger as he led her through several corridors until they came to a small private chapel. He opened the door for her and she entered inside. The door closed softly behind her, leaving her alone or so she thought, until she saw the king kneeling to one side of the altar.

She approached him slowly, looking around her as she did so. The chapel was ornately decorated and quite breath taking.

"Pray with me, Miss Robins," the king ordered her, his voice hushed.

She knelt down beside him and, clasping her hands together, closed her eyes.

"We will not be disturbed here," the king said. "Do you have any more letters for me or information?"

"There has been nothing, Your Majesty."

She felt his eyes upon hers and opened her own, angling her head to catch his gaze.

"I want you to find out when next she will be visiting him. Can you do that?"

Lydia swallowed hard. "I have gained her trust. Perhaps I can somehow find out but it may be difficult."

"I am certain you will find a way." He stood up and held out his hand to her. He helped her rise and she stood before him uncertainly. She could feel her heart hammering in her chest but his next words left her breathless. "If you wished, you could hold a much higher position than you do now."

She licked her lips nervously. "H-how do you mean, Your Majesty?"

"Say the word and everything you have ever dreamt of will be yours." He looked deep into her eyes. "Everything."

She knew exactly what he meant and as handsome and regal as he was, she knew she would never take him up on his offer.

He lifted his hand and ran his finger over her bottom lip. "I have rarely felt such a need for a woman as I have you, Miss Robins."

"I thank Your Majesty, but I—"

He hushed her next words, placing his finger over her lips. "I will give you time to think on it but do not make me wait too long." He took her hand and turned it over, kissing the soft skin on her palm. "Return to the queen, Miss Robins. We will talk anon."

She curtseyed and almost ran from the chapel, her mind in a whirl. Lord Danbye's words came back to her and she realised he had been quite right. What the devil was she going to do now, though?

LYDIA HAD a restless night and barely slept. In the morning, the queen noted immediately that she was not looking her best.

"Miss Robins, you have dark circles beneath your eyes. Has someone been keeping you up late?"

Lydia's eyes shot to hers. "No, Your Majesty, I simply could not sleep properly last night. I think it was just a little too warm in our room."

The queen looked across to Cecily, who had just entered the room, holding a small box of jewellery. "Miss Walters, did you find your room too hot last night?"

"Not particularly, Your Majesty. Why do you ask?"

"Miss Robins did not sleep at all well due to the heat coming from your room."

"Oh." Cecily looked at Lydia, wondering what was going on.

All became clear when the queen added, "It would have nothing to do with Lord Danbye perchance, Miss Robins?"

Lydia blushed beet red. "Lord Danbye? I know not what you imply?"

Queen Catherine raised an eyebrow. "I have been told that you and he have visited each other's rooms on occasion. Is he your lover, Miss Robins?"

Lydia gasped involuntarily but before she could reply, the queen laughed out loud softly. "I am sorry to tease you. Forgive me?"

God's bones, there were spies everywhere. How had she found out that Lord Danbye had visited her. Despite the queen saying she was just teasing her, Lydia had the urge to redeem herself.

"Lord Danbye is watching over both Cecily and me whilst we are here. He feels the need to protect us should the occasion arise. He is a close friend of the family."

"You need not explain, Miss Robins. I have noted on many an occasion how chivalrous Lord Danbye can be," said the queen.

Lydia stopped herself from pulling a face. Yes, Lord Danbye could be chivalrous but not when he was spanking her bottom. Then he was far from chivalrous!

The queen raised her hand and waved Cecily over. "Now, Cecily, bring the jewellery to me. I must decide what to wear today."

With the queen's attention on her jewellery, Lady Castlemaine chose that moment to pull Lydia to one side. "Why do you play with a mere dog when you can have a lion?" she enquired, her voice low so the queen couldn't hear.

Lydia did her best not to look irritated but failed. She knew exactly what Lady Castlemaine was implying but she was so wrong. Lord Danbye had no interest in her and she had no interest in the king.

Lady Castlemaine whispered, "Give the king what he wants and he shall be yours to command."

"How do you know what the king wants?"

"I see everything that goes on in this court and I know, for certain, the king has fallen for you."

"That may be so, but I do not wish to give myself to him!" Lydia snapped.

"Listen to me, girl, you will never again have a king at your feet. This opportunity has presented itself and you must act upon it," she said, her voice in earnest.

"That is for me to decide, Lady Castlemaine. Now if you will excuse me, I must see to the queen's wardrobe."

She excused herself and escaped to the wardrobe room where she sat down on a stool and placed her head in her hands. What on earth was going on? As if she didn't have enough to worry about, now she would have to concern herself with people watching her and Lord Danbye's every move. God's bones!

And why was Lady Castlemaine so insistent on her bedding the king? Surely, that was a position filled not only by her but by Louise de Keroualle. Something was afoot and she liked it not.

A FEW DAYS passed and thankfully, Lydia did not encounter the king. There were rumours that a man called Thomas Blood had made an attempt to steal the crown jewels. A daring act indeed and now captured, the king had yet to decide his fate.

Lydia was thankful that at least it was keeping the king occupied and for now, she didn't have to inform him of her choice not to become his mistress.

It worried her that he would react badly. After all, he was the king. He could have anything he wanted. But be that as it may, she had no desire to sleep with him and would tell him so, whatever the consequences would be.

She had only seen Lord Danbye from a distance since their last meeting. There was talk of another Dutch war and it was keeping the court officials on their toes with plenty to discuss and organise. She supposed Lord Danbye would have little time to himself with such important decisions to make, but she found she missed him.

As arrogant and overbearing as he could sometimes be, she missed his strong presence. Being held accountable for her actions, somehow made her feel safe. He was sincere in his intentions and one could almost think he was in love with her. But would a suitor want to chastise her so often as Lord Danbye seemed to do?

Puzzled, she scooped up the basket containing the queen's dirty laundry and headed off down the stairs towards the laundry room. It wasn't a task she enjoyed and she very much doubted the women who worked there enjoyed it, either. The room was always full of steam emanating from the big vats of hot water full of clothing. Thankfully she only had to drop the laundry off and collect it, the thought of working there was dreadful and she pitied those who did.

After dropping the basket off and hastily leaving the room, she paused a moment to adjust the buckle on her shoe. Whilst bending down, she became aware of hushed talking coming from a door to her right. It was slightly ajar and her ears instantly pricked up when she heard Lady Castlemaine's name mentioned.

Sidling nearer, she pretended to still adjust her buckle whilst listening intently to the conversation. What she heard made her eyes widen. It was John Churchill and he was telling someone about what he and Lady Castlemaine got up to between the sheets. Her cheeks blushed at the language he was using and she went to walk off but quickly stopped when the man he was talking to asked when John would be seeing her again.

"Tonight. I am going to her chamber at midnight. I would rather play cards with you and Blenheim but without her five hundred pounds, I would have nothing to gamble with anyway."

"I thought you invested it?"

"Yes, most of it. But my expenses at court are quite high and father's allowance hardly covers them, so I had to keep some back. You never know, I might get more out of her yet!"

Both men laughed and Lydia chose that moment to hurry away. So Lady Castlemaine paid him for his services. What news indeed and something the king would wish to know about. Instead of going back to the queen's chambers, she changed course towards the king's rooms. The guards outside raised an eyebrow when she asked to see him.

"Wait here," one of them said and disappeared into the room.

Lydia shuffled her feet uncomfortably as the other guard openly scrutinised her. Heaven knew what he was thinking. The door opened again and the first guard stood aside so she could enter.

The king was waiting for her by one of the leaded windows. He smiled warmly and beckoned her forward. Lydia was thankful when she realised they were alone.

"Miss Robins, for what do I owe the pleasure?"

"I have news for you about Lady Castlemaine, Your Majesty."

"And there I was thinking you had come to give me your decision."

"Oh!" Lydia blushed profusely.

"Tell me what news you have first."

She explained to him about the conversation she had overheard and his face grew dark, especially when she mentioned the money.

"So she uses my generosity to pay for her lovers. She has gone too far." He placed his hands behind his back and looked out of the window. "The people hate her and I think this time, they are right. She has overstepped a line."

"Why do people hate her so?" Lydia asked.

"She meddles in affairs that do not concern her. It has been brewing for a long time but I cannot excuse her behaviour any longer. I will see her gone from court."

As much as she didn't like Lady Castlemaine, to know her position at court would soon be severed was a little harsh, but as she was learning, life at court was not easy.

The king's face softened when he turned around and saw the look of concern on her face. "Do not worry for her. She is extremely versatile and will no doubt soon find another niche in life. I have given her enough money and houses to ensure her lifestyle will not suffer."

He walked over and took her hand. "I thank you for the information but perhaps, now, you will give me your answer?"

Lydia swallowed hard and despite being nervous, she was determined to tell him her true feelings. "I thank Your Majesty for such an offer, but I am not ready to take on such a position. I hope you understand."

He stroked her face with the back of his hand. "Perhaps you are not ready now but I have hope you will be soon. I will not give up on you, Miss Robins."

She kept quiet, unsure of what to say, or indeed what she could say, to dissuade him from thinking they would ever be together.

He dropped his hand. "Very well, Miss Robins. Go back to your duties but think upon my words."

She curtseyed and headed back to the queen's rooms, wondering what action the king would take with Lady Castlemaine.

∼

*That night...*

Lady Castlemaine was sound asleep. After an evening of debauchery with her current favourite bed partner, John Churchill, a dashing young officer, she was completely worn out, her body sated and languorous.

When her bedchamber door opened, she never stirred. Neither did she stir when someone sat down on the edge of her bed. She only awoke when she felt a finger lightly stroke her face. She moaned softly and muttered, "Have you not had enough, my darling?"

"No," said the king. "Not nearly enough, it would seem!"

Her eyes flew open and she instantly awoke. "Your Majesty!"

But the king's eyes were not upon her, they were resting on the slumbering form next to her. Reaching over, he pulled down the covers.

John Churchill awoke instantly as the cold draught hit his naked body. Blearily, he looked up, and when he saw who had awoken him, he went into a full-blown panic.

"Oh! Your Majesty!" He leapt up from the bed and scrambled to one corner, grabbing his pile of clothes in one smooth move. Crouching down, he attempted to hide his nudity and buried his head in his hands, shamefaced.

"What are you doing here, John Churchill?" the king asked him. "Do you fancy yourself in love with my Lady Castlemaine?"

John darted a look at Lady Castlemaine before replying, "In truth, I have little feeling for her but she was most insistent, and I have been taught that a gentleman should never be impolite."

The king laughed, especially when he noted the look of outrage on Lady Castlemaine's face and noted, "She is also generous to her lovers, is she not? How much did she give you?"

"Five hundred pounds," John admitted quietly. He made no attempt to hide the fact.

The king raised his eyebrows. "A handsome sum! What have you done with the money?"

"Invested it in a pension, Your Majesty," he whispered.

"Goodness! A wise move for such a young man." He stared at his bowed head and added, "Well then, I forgive you. A young man must have something to live on, after all." He waved his hand at him. "Away with you."

John quickly fled the room, leaving a silence in his wake.

The king quietly assessed Lady Castlemaine and she raised her chin a little, asking, "What are you doing here? You have not sought my bed in weeks."

"I came to see for myself what is going on."

"You knew about John?"

He nodded. Lady Castlemaine's eyes narrowed. "From whom?"

"It is of no consequence. But know this, I wish you to leave. Go to your house in Nonsuch and leave us in peace. My patience is exhausted."

Lady Castlemaine leapt up from the bed, anger emanating from every pore. "I will not be usurped by that French whore, Louise, or that little upstart Lydia Robins!"

King Charles' temper erupted. "Enough! Neither of those women deserve your wrath."

Lady Castlemaine's eyes narrowed. "Lydia Robins has no interest in you. She is having an affair with Lord Danbye."

King Charles paused as her words sank in. "Lord Danbye?"

Seeing as she had caught his attention, Lady Castlemaine embellished her words. "Yes, it is common knowledge that the two of them share a bed. She is not worthy of the honour of sharing yours."

"And you are? After taking that young letch into your bed?"

"I only took him to my bed because you have been neglecting me." Her famous temper rose as she added, "After giving you six children, this is how you treat me?"

"I treated you well—it is you who has gone too far. I forgave you your ambition and your greed, but you meddle in court affairs. You just cannot help yourself and I am sick of it, as is everyone."

He turned his back on her and, opening the door, called to one of her servants. "Have Lady Castlemaine's goods packed, she is leaving."

"I am not!" Lady Castlemaine protested loudly. "I will not go!"

Charles turned back to her. "I give you no choice." He gave her a hard stare. "All I ask is that you live quietly and cause me no more grief; do that and I care not who you love."

He left her rooms without a backward glance and in that moment Lady Castlemaine realised she had lost the king's love forever.

# CHAPTER 6

*L*ord Danbye rubbed the back of his neck wearily. He had been sat around the king's table for several hours, discussing the Dutch and the possible threat of a third Anglo-Dutch war.

Parliament were decidedly unenthusiastic about a new war, having already had two wars with the Dutch within the last twenty years. War was costly, not only to life but to England's purse. But King Charles was adamant.

It led to a lengthy meeting between parliament, the king, and his advisors, of which Lord Danbye was included. There were a lot of raised voices and heated arguments and the atmosphere in the room became extremely tense.

By the time the king called an end to the meeting, little had been decided and the consensus was that they would convene another day. Lord Danbye wondered if perhaps the king thought parliament would reconsider their objections and change their minds. In all truth, he doubted it. Once parliament dug their heels in, it was hard to get them to change their mind.

As everyone began to filter out of the room, King Charles asked Lord Danbye to remain behind. When the room was empty and they were alone, the king sat back in his chair and studied him.

"I have learned that Miss Robins and you have a liaison."

Whatever Lord Danbye thought the king was going to ask, it wasn't that. He frowned and replied truthfully, "No, Your Majesty, we do not. Who told you such a thing?"

"Lady Castlemaine swears by it, and although she is not exactly trustworthy, I took her at her word and made some enquiries myself." He paused and looked at him astutely. "There is much talk around court that you and she are romantically involved."

Lord Danbye raised his eyebrows. "I assure you we are not. I care very much for her, but I believe my feelings are unrequited."

"Do you love her?"

"In all truth, yes."

"Then marry her. Whether your relationship, whatever that may be, is innocent or not, it matters not. Court gossip has paired you two together and if you care for her as you say you do, you would do best to give her your name and your protection." He tapped his fingers on the table. "I will be honest with you, Lord Danbye. Lady Castlemaine has noticed that Miss Robins has caught my eye and I will not deny it. She is a beautiful girl. But the fact is that even though Lady Castlemaine has left my court, her spies remain everywhere and I think life for Miss Robins could become, shall we say, difficult."

"I see." Lord Danbye nodded his head. Lady Castlemaine was a force to be reckoned with and Lydia's reputation would be in shreds were he not to marry her. He could take her away from court, back to a quiet life in Barnham before Lady Castlemaine's spite could fan the flames of this idle gossip that surrounded them.

Whether Lydia would accept his proposal remained to be seen.

"I suggest you inform Miss Robins of your intention at the

earliest opportunity. Lady Castlemaine is in high dudgeon and it is only a matter of time before she lets loose her tongue."

"Very well. I thank you for warning me."

"I depend on my friends to deal with me honestly, Lord Danbye which is why I return the compliment."

Lord Danbye left the room and headed off to his own quarters. He would spruce himself up and invite Lydia to his rooms that very night. The sooner he took her away from court, the better.

LYDIA SAT in front of her dressing table in her room, whilst Cecily helped style her hair. They were to attend a ball that night to celebrate the summer solstice. It was a gorgeously warm evening and they had been told to expect a lavish affair, both inside the court and outside in the extensive grounds.

Cecily was rather excited. "I wonder what gown Louise de Keroualle will be wearing? She has the most exquisite taste."

"You will look just as splendid, Cecily, if not more so. The queen has provided both of us with new gowns and I have to say that they are quite beautiful."

Cecily slipped the last pin in Lydia's hair and looked at her in the mirror. "There, what do you think?"

She had given her a centre parting with a tiny braid of hair across the top and long ringlets either side, pulled up with pale blue ribbons to match her dress. She shook her head and the curls bounced softly.

"It is perfect. Now, let me do yours."

They changed position and Lydia began to deftly untie the cloth ribbons until Cecily's hair was a mass of curls. "Now to tame it!" She laughed.

She soon had Cecily's hair looking as neat and tidy as her

own except Cecily had cream-coloured ribbons to match her dress.

"There. We are both ready," she declared.

Lydia walked over to her bed and just as she went to pick up her reticule and fan, she noticed a note on the floor by their door. She frowned and walking over, she picked it up. It was sealed with wax and on the front it had her name on it.

"That is odd, someone has slipped a note under the door. I never heard anyone knock, did you?"

Cecily frowned. "No. Is it for you or me?"

"Me." Lydia quickly broke the seal and opened the folded letter.

"Who is it from?" Cecily asked, walking over.

Lydia glanced down to the bottom. "Lady Castlemaine. I wonder why she is writing to me?"

"Perhaps she wishes to leave you with some parting advice, now that she has left the queen's services," Cecily wondered.

Lydia held the letter out so they could both read it and within moments they were both open mouthed as they noted the contents. Cecily was the first to respond, "By the rood, she accuses you of snooping on her private affairs and informing the king!"

"How on earth did she find out it was me?" Lydia breathed nervously.

Cecily's eyes nearly popped out of her head and she gasped, "You mean it is true? You spied on her?"

Lydia nodded. "The king asked me to do it. It was not my choice, believe me."

"God's bones, Lydia. She is openly hostile in that letter. Look at this line," she tapped her finger on the paper, "*I will make your life hell*. Upon my word, she is not a person to take lightly! What will you do?"

"She is no longer at court, so her threats are empty," Lydia said with bravado. "The queen said herself that she has gone to Somerset House. What can she do to me from there?"

"I would not put anything past that woman," Cecily warned her. "Perhaps you should show her letter to the king. He will be able to protect you. I do not wish to worry you, but I have heard that people have been poisoned for lesser deeds than she has accused you of."

"God's bones, Cecily! You are supposed to reassure me, not make me feel worse."

Cecily shrugged her shoulders. "I only seek to caution you. Her words are vitriolic to say the least."

Lydia worried her bottom lip with her teeth and read the note again, agreeing, "Yes, in all truth, they are. The king did assure me that she could do me no harm but I beg to differ. I will keep this note in my reticule and if an opportunity to tell the king presents itself tonight, then I will show him. He will know what to do."

LYDIA AND CECILY, along with the other ladies in waiting, walked behind Queen Catherine as she presented herself at the ball. The gardens had been decorated beautifully with garlands and lit torches, creating an ambient atmosphere. The king approached Catherine and took her hand.

"You look beautiful this evening, madam," he complimented her. "Come, sit with me by the pond."

He led her towards a long, padded bench and she settled herself beside him. They seemed so content in one another's company that Lydia wondered why he had the need for other women. But it was not her place to wonder why. Queen Catherine obviously knew of his mistresses, he certainly did little to hide it, so she must be a very tolerant woman. Lydia knew if she were in her place, she would never accept him taking other women into his bed. She would end up divorcing him. Thank goodness she wasn't a queen.

She followed Cecily as she walked over to the other side of the pond. There was a pretty fountain in the middle and the water cascading down was quite mesmerising.

One of the staff appeared by their side, a tray in his hands containing small glasses of punch. Lydia declined but Cecily happily took one.

"That is very strong, Cecily," she cautioned.

Cecily waved her hand in the air dismissively and took a sip, closing her eyes with delight as she sampled the heady drink. "You should have one, Lydia."

"No, she should not," drawled a deep voice nearby. It was Lord Danbye. He looked particularly handsome tonight and his waistcoat, in pale blue, matched her dress perfectly.

She drew her eyes away from his physique and raised an indignant eyebrow. "That is not for you to decide, Lord Danbye."

"Considering the effect it had on you last time, I think it is." Another member of staff passed by with a tray of wine and he reached out and took two glasses. "You will find this far more tolerable, I assure you," he told her.

She accepted the glass and sipped a little. Even though he was a little presumptuous, she knew his was the voice of reason as the wine tasted silky smooth on her tongue. She smiled at him. "Once again, you make a valid point." she conceded, "it is the better choice."

His eyes crinkled. "Ah, she submits to my greater knowledge."

Lydia snorted softly. "Only this once. Do not let it go to your head."

"I would never do that, Miss Robins." He chuckled. "I came over to ask if you would allow me the pleasure of a dance this evening?"

"That would be lovely," she replied honestly. For a big man, he was extremely agile and she had enjoyed dancing with him previously.

"Also I wish to speak with you. Perhaps, later, when the ball finishes?" he added.

"Of course. May I ask what it is about?"

"It will keep until later. I would rather we were alone." He looked pointedly at Cecily. Although her attention was taken up with something else, she was standing too close not to overhear their conversation.

"Excuse me, Miss Robins. Lord Peterson is gesturing to me. Until later." He raised her hand and kissed the soft skin. His lips were firm and she instantly wondered what it would feel like to kiss him. Startled at where her thoughts were leading her, she felt her face flush with desire.

Lord Danbye's eyes darkened and took on an almost hungry expression as he seemed to notice the heat steal over her cheeks. Lydia had never seen him look at her so before, and for a moment she was transfixed. Did he feel the same?

But she had no time to dwell on it then, as he lowered her hand and walked over to Lord Peterson. Lydia took a mouthful of wine and let the warming liquid seep down her throat. Good Lord, his effect on her seemed to be deepening.

She suddenly realised Cecily was staring at her oddly. "Do you still maintain that those rumours about you and Lord Danbye are falsehoods?" she enquired, her eyes sparkling with interest.

"Of course, they are. Why do you ask?"

"Oh, nothing."

Lydia started to get irritated, "Do not 'oh nothing' me! What are you implying?"

Cecily grinned. "From what I have just witnessed, dearest Lydia, I do declare that both of you are in love with one another. Any fool can see it."

"No, we are not. You are reading far too much into it. As for fools—are you still playing with your guard?"

"There is no need to be irksome, I am only telling you what I see. As for John Russell, then yes, I am still seeing him." She twiddled with a strand of hair absently before blurting out, "He has declared himself to me, you know."

Lydia's eyes widened and she gasped, "Tell me you refused."

"Of course, I did." Cecily gave a wistful sigh. "Although I would have loved to have said otherwise."

"I am quite certain your parents would have something to say on the matter."

"Indeed they would, but they do not know him like I do. If only he had a title. Life is unfair, Lydia. I find someone I love and I cannot have him." She pulled a face of disappointment. "I just hope that when the time comes, they do not try to marry me off to some cantankerous old stinkpot."

Lydia clapped a hand over her mouth to stifle her laughter. "Cecily, I am certain you would let them know exactly what you thought if they even dared to try."

Cecily giggled back. "Ah, yes, I most certainly would. Oh well, for now I will have to console myself with stolen kisses."

Lydia tutted disapprovingly but refrained from saying anything further on the matter. Instead, she pulled lightly on Cecily's sleeve and said, "Come, let us go and see what food has been prepared. I find I am quite famished."

Cecily needed no persuading and the two girls made their way to the food hall.

THE PALACE CHEFS had prepared a lavish feast for the guests and both girls helped themselves to the delicious food. There was everything from thinly sliced meats to perfect little pastries, both sweet and savoury, all laid out on a long table at the side of the room.

A little while later, Cecily excused herself to go to the privy chamber and left Lydia alone for a moment.

Reaching for one of the succulent little pastries, Lydia had just taken a bite when she heard a loud, meaningful cough behind her. She spun around and found herself confronted by none other than Lady Castlemaine. Her face was pinched and her eyes contained nothing but malice.

Realising the hostility was directed at her, Lydia almost choked on the food, in her haste to swallow it.

"Lady Castlemaine," Lydia acknowledged, curtseying nervously. What the devil was she doing here? According to the king and queen, she had left court and retired to Somerset House.

When she looked up, several other people had gathered around them, as if sensing something untoward was about to happen. Lydia immediately recalled Lady Castlemaine's letter and a sense of danger overwhelmed her.

"Miss Robins," Lady Castlemaine began. Her voice was sugary sweet but her eyes were still full of venom. "I am surprised to see you in such a beautiful dress, for the last time I saw you, you were quite naked."

"I beg your pardon?" Lydia could hardly believe what she was hearing and blushed to her roots.

Lady Castlemaine gave a harsh laugh. "Come now, Miss Robins, you know very well what I am referring to." She tapped her on the arm with her fan. "Why, you cannot have forgotten already. It was only two days ago."

Lydia had never been so embarrassed in her life. A couple of the women behind Lady Castlemaine began to titter, their eyes alight with amusement.

"I assure you, I know not what you mean!" she protested.

"Come now, it was when I caught you in Lord Danbye's arms,

down by the summer house. I do apologise for interrupting you both—I do hope he was able to rise to the occasion once you returned to his bedroom?"

The women openly laughed, ridiculing her and Lydia's mouth fell open. "Lord Danbye?" She gasped, "I fear you have mistaken me for someone else, Lady Castlemaine."

"Oh no, my dear. I know very well what I saw. You may deny it all you like but everyone already knows that you and he are involved." She looked about her, her voice rising slightly in order to gain even more attention.

Lydia straightened her back, trying not to let her intimidate her. "By the rood, we are not!"

"Do not deny it, my dear. It does you no good." She waved her hand about, encompassing the crowd, "Everyone knows you are no longer the innocent you claim to be."

"You have gone too far, Lady Castlemaine!" Lydia accused her angrily.

"No, I think you will find it is you who has gone too far, Miss Robins." Her eyes glittered with spite, her lips thinning with anger.

"If you seek to besmirch my name, then you cannot, for these claims are false." Lydia balled her fists by her side, angry and embarrassed at being so falsely and publicly accused.

"You see how her cheeks flush with guilt?" Lady Castlemaine said, her eyes full of malice. "You are a trollop, my dear, admit it. I think it is about time you left court and returned to your home."

"Enough, Lady Castlemaine!" a deep voice admonished her. It was the king, and just by taking one look at his face, Lydia knew he was outraged. She hadn't noticed him approach and neither, apparently, had Lady Castlemaine who immediately curtseyed.

The king's face remained set, his eyes, however, were dark and angry. "Isn't it about time you retired, Lady Castlemaine?"

"Your Majesty, I was simply telling everyone—"

He held up his hand, interrupting her. "It is not your place to tell anyone anything, and I have no wish to know, either. You were not invited to this ball so I suggest you leave now of your own accord." The implied threat was enough to make Lady Castlemaine's eyes widen. If she didn't leave on her own, she would be escorted out and that would be highly embarrassing. With what little dignity she had left, she curtseyed again and promptly walked away, her small entourage following behind.

Lydia had never been so relieved in her life. Her cheeks were still flaming when she looked up at the king. His eyes were full of sympathy.

"My dear, would you honour me with a dance?"

Blinking away tears of mortification, she nodded and took his offered arm as he led her away from the small crowd that had gathered. Inclining his head towards hers, he whispered, "I am sorry you had to endure Lady Castlemaine's acid tongue. It will not happen again."

Lydia could tell from his tone that Lady Castlemaine would not find it so easy to enter Whitehall in the future, if ever. Hopefully the king's public dressing down would make her rethink her ways and keep to Somerset House.

"Thank you, Your Majesty," she said in a small voice.

The king stopped for a moment, and placing his mouth near her ear, he said, "Lord Danbye wishes to speak with you and I strongly advise you to think very carefully upon his words."

"He has spoken to you?"

"Indeed, he has. I shall say no more for it is his words you must hear."

"Oh." Lydia thought hard. What could he possibly wish to speak to her about? An idea formed in her mind and she immediately dismissed it, but then it crept back in again. What if he wished to ask for her hand in marriage? Oh, lord, what would she say? Did she want to have such a disciplinarian for a husband?

She had no more time to dwell on the matter, however, before the king was leading her onto the dance area where he hoped to take her mind off the horrendous encounter she had just endured.

# CHAPTER 7

Throughout the dance, Lydia could feel several eyes upon her and try as she might to ignore them, she couldn't help overhearing the heavy whispers as they reached her ears.

*"One never would have guessed—she looks so innocent!"*

*"I declare, she is most brazen!"*

*"They say she has given herself to the king—'tis how she gained her position."*

Lydia's face flamed with embarrassment. Good lord, Lady Castlemaine had done a wondrous job of tarnishing her name, and being such a high-ranking member of the court, most of them believed her falsehoods. For why would they believe Lydia Robins who was but a newcomer?

What worried Lydia the most was how the queen might react when the unfounded gossip reached her ears. For someone would surely tell her. What if she wished to dismiss her from her employ? She would have to return home with her tail between her legs. Her mother and father would be ashamed. She closed her eyes for a moment, her despair evident.

"Do not look so glum, Miss Robins. For when one door closes, another will open."

She opened her eyes and looked at the king quizzically, waiting for him to elaborate but he just gave her a reassuring smile and as the dance ended, he turned her around and gently nudged her forward towards Lord Danbye, who was waiting for her to one side.

~

NEWS OF LADY Castlemaine's behaviour had reached Lord Danbye whilst he was in the middle of a game of cards with Lord Peterson and several others.

Shocked but not surprised, he immediately threw his cards down, forfeiting the game. Even though he had a good hand and would well have won, his only concern was to offer his support to Lydia, who was no doubt mortified.

As annoyed as he was when he heard what Lydia had been accused of, he knew his reputation would not be tarnished but Lydia's would undoubtedly be sullied. It was something he had feared and the king had warned him of.

Anxiously, he had returned to the main hall and looked around, searching for Lydia. He had felt immensely relieved when he found her in the arms of the king, knowing that no one would dare say anything untoward whilst she was under his protection.

He walked over and stood at the edge of the dance area. King Charles immediately noticed him and they exchanged meaningful glances. When the music ended, the king delivered Lydia straight into his arms.

"I suggest we go somewhere quiet, Miss Robins." Her eyes were wide in her face and he could feel her distress. He held his arm out for her and she settled her small hand on his sleeve, not saying a word.

He couldn't help but admire the way she held her head up high as they exited the hall. She might be mortified on the inside, but she wasn't going to show it to the others present. She was a strong little thing and he was glad for it.

Walking along the torch lit corridors, neither said a word, both acutely conscious that anything they had to say was for their ears only. There was enough gossip already without adding to it.

Reaching his rooms, he took out his key and unlocked the door. Turning the handle, he pushed it open and ushered her gently inside, before closing it firmly behind himself.

She immediately turned around and faced him, her anger and distress now evident. "Did you hear what happened?" she exclaimed, throwing her arms out wide. "That woman is an abomination."

He shook his head. "Her conduct was disgraceful. It has done her no favours." He placed his large hands on her slender arms and led her over to a chair. "Sit down whilst I light some candles. I wish to see you more clearly. Then we can converse properly."

She did as he bid and remained quiet, staring into the flames and watching the small embers disappear into the chimney, whilst Lord Danbye lit several candles around the room, softly illuminating the plush decor.

Returning to her side, he placed a comforting hand on her shoulder and reiterating the king's words, he said, "It will never happen again."

Lydia's hands shot up to her face, covering her cheeks. "It was so embarrassing! She accused you and me of... of..."

Lord Danbye took her hand and drew her up out of the chair. Placing his strong arms around her, he embraced her gently. "She is a malicious woman, and now she is no longer the king's favourite, she seeks to taint anyone who gains the king's attention."

Lydia closed her eyes and took comfort in Lord Danbye's

strength. He smelled divine. "I admit he did ask me to become his mistress, but I declined. She has nothing to fear from me in that way." She sighed heavily. "The truth of the matter is that she has found out that I spied on her for the king."

Lord Danbye's eyebrows nearly reached his hairline and he pulled away so he could see her face. "No wonder she is vexed. I am surprised he asked you to do such a thing."

"He said he trusted me." She looked up at him, her big blue eyes full of innocence.

"Yes, that I can see. There are many in court who are the complete opposite."

"She sent me a note. I have it here." She stepped out of his embrace and reaching into her bodice, drew out the small, folded letter which she handed to him. "I received it just before we left our room."

Lord Danbye opened it and quickly scanned the contents, his face growing grim the more he read. "She is a pathetic woman, seeking to destroy others' happiness. A conniving witch."

"Do you think the queen will still wish me to serve her should she hear of these accusations?"

"I know not, but in truth, I have something to say that affects your future. Come, take a seat."

He held his hand out towards the armchair and she perched on the edge of the seat, wondering if her intuition was right and that he would now declare himself.

He studied her intensely before speaking. "I will come straight to the point, Miss Robins. I wish to marry you."

Lydia sucked in a small breath and went to speak, but he held up a hand, silencing her. "Before you say yea or nay, let me continue." He paced the rug in front of her, his hands clasped behind his back. "I have had feelings towards you for quite a while now but because of our age difference, I did not pursue them. But now, given the situation we find ourselves in, I wonder if perhaps you would consider it? My name will protect you from any gossip that will ensue. They will have nothing to talk about as we will be married and their attention will take another path. We will soon be forgotten."

He stopped pacing and looked at her. "You know already that I am wealthy. You will want for nothing."

Lydia searched his face. "Do you love me?"

"Yes, I confess I do. You are a wilful madam on occasion, but you are also sweet and charming when you want to be. So, yes, I do love you."

What he offered her was most tempting. She would have a spacious home, a handsome man who loved her, and she would also be right near her parents, so visiting often would not be a problem. But did she love him? She frowned, thinking hard. He did make her heart flutter but was that enough to spend a life-time with someone?

He noticed her hesitation and spoke softly, "If you do not love me, then I will not pressure you. I simply seek to protect you."

She tilted her head and asked him, "Would you still think to chastise me if we marry?"

He gave a low chuckle. "Yes, I most certainly will."

Lydia made a small moue with her mouth and her eyebrows lowered. "But as a wife, I should be revered surely?"

He shook his head and folded his thickly muscled arms across his broad chest. "You will be revered, but if you behave badly, you will be punished. You know by now, that I have little tolerance for mischief." He quirked an eyebrow and added, "But if you behave, then you will have no concerns on that account, will you?"

Lydia placed a finger on her bottom lip and thought hard upon his words. Could she behave, and more to the point, did she *want* to behave? Something about going over his strong thighs stirred emotions in her that she didn't quite understand. The secret place between her thighs seemed to come alive when his large hand spanked her bare bottom. No one else made her feel that way and in truth, if that was love, then yes, she did love him.

Lydia focussed her gaze on him and realized that no other man would do. He was dominant but fair, and she knew instinctively that her heart was already his. She smiled softly. "Yes, Lord Danbye, I will marry you."

He reached out and, taking her hand, drew her up against him, wrapping his strong arms around her once more. "You have made me a very happy man, Lydia Robins."

He cupped his hand against her cheek and kissed her gently on the lips. His touch sent a frisson of excitement rippling through her and sighing with pleasure, she parted her mouth invitingly, wanting more. She had wondered what it would feel like to kiss him and now she intended to find out.

He moulded her body to his and intensified their kiss, his lips firmly meshing with hers. It left Lydia breathless and slightly giddy with desire.

He pulled away and looked at her lovingly, "I promise I will make you happy, Lydia."

"And I promise to be a dutiful wife, my lord, but must we not ask the queen's permission before we marry, not forgetting my parents?"

"Yes, but I am certain they will all agree. The king has already given his permission, so the queen should have no objection. I will ask her on the morrow. As for your parents, they know my character, my wealth and position—I am certain they will have no objections."

He planted a kiss on her soft lips. "Now, my beauty, I will escort you back to your room and in the morning, after I have spoken with Queen Catherine, we shall tell everyone of our intention. The sooner I get you back to Barnham, the better."

~

LYDIA ARRIVED BACK to her room, to find Cecily was already there. She was propped up in bed with a silly smile on her face. Lord Danbye had already taken his leave once he had delivered her safely to her room.

"You look happy," Lydia noted, sitting down on the end of her own bed and reaching down to take her buckled shoes off.

Cecily hiccoughed. "I am, verily so."

Lydia glanced over her shoulder at her, noticing how flushed her cheeks were. "How many glasses of that punch did you imbibe, Cecily?"

"I do not remember." Cecily giggled before hiccoughing again. "But I did enjoy the taste."

"I suppose you heard what was said earlier?"

Cecily's eyes widened and as inebriated as she was, she still managed to muster a look of concern. "Indeed, I did! Why, if I had been there, I would have knocked her out." She swung a fist in the air rather limply, and Lydia shook her head.

"No, you would not have. Ladies do not act in such a manner."

"No, truly, I would have and hang the consequences!" Cecily drawled. "That woman is trouble."

"On that, we agree. The king told her to leave. She was not even invited in the first place. She just came here to make mischief, an odious woman."

"What are you going to do?" Cecily hiccoughed again and her eyelids drooped.

"I will tell you in the morning when you are more alert. I think the best thing for you is to get some sleep."

Cecily shook her head and then immediately regretted it, holding a hand up to her forehead and grimacing. "Ew, my head is spinning."

"Too much punch." Lydia noted, pulling a face. "Next time, take the wine instead."

"Never! Now tell me, what do you intend to do? *Hic* I must know before I fall asleep."

Lydia smiled with amusement. "I will tell you, but you will not remember in the morning anyway." She threw her shoes next to the bed and began to roll down her stockings. "Lord Danbye has proposed to me and I have accepted."

For a moment, Cecily lay in shocked silence before blinking rapidly and sitting bolt upright. "You are going to marry him?"

Lydia nodded and stood up, beginning to unpin her bodice.

"Are you leaving court? Of course, you are leaving court! But when? God's bones! What am I supposed to do without you here?" She was beginning to babble.

"Calm down, Cecily. I am not certain when we will leave—it depends on what the queen has to say. And you will do perfectly well without me. You have made many friends and if they appoint someone to replace me, they will share this room with you and all will be well."

'I am not staying here without you," Cecily said adamantly, her upper body swaying slightly.

"You cannot mean that." Lydia tutted loudly. "You are not thinking straight."

"I can. I do!" Cecily seemed to be sobering up fast. She slipped her legs from beneath the coverlet and padded over to the bureau, clad in her long nightdress. "I am going to send a note to John Russell."

Lydia took off her bodice and stared at Cecily, not liking where their conversation was heading. "Why do you wish to contact him?"

"If you can get married, so can I! He has asked me, and now I am going to say yes."

Lydia hurried over to her, her eyes wide. "You cannot, Cecily! He is just a guard. Your parents will disown you," she said in a rush. "Please, I beg you, do not be so hasty. Get some sleep and in the morning you will think more clearly."

"My heart belongs to him, Lydia. No, my mind is made up. Do not try to stop me, and do not dare tell anyone."

"But, Cecily, where will you live? What will you live on? His wage will not keep you in the manner you have been accustomed to." She exclaimed, "Is your love really worth it?"

Cecily turned to her, eyes alight with excitement, and said, "Yes, I would rather have a life with him and true love than a life without either."

"God's bones, Cecily. I do not envy you when your parents find out."

"They will not find out until I am married. Promise me that you will say nothing."

Lydia looked at her hard. She had clearly had too much punch and wasn't thinking straight. She placed her hands on her hips and nodded slowly. "I will say nothing unless asked. But I still think you are acting in haste."

"I do not care! I am going to marry him and no one can stop me."

Lydia realised that in Cecily's current mood, there was nothing more she could say to dissuade her so she walked back to her bed, removed the rest of her clothing, and slipped on a long white nightdress. She glanced over at Cecily, who was now seated at the table writing a note to her beloved, the quill flying over the parchment at a rapid pace. Goodness knows what she was writing or if it even made sense due to her current inebriation.

Shrugging her slender shoulders, Lydia climbed wearily into her bed and closed her eyes. It had been a long day and she was mentally worn out. Tomorrow could prove to be just as tiring; she would have to wait and see. It took a long time to fall asleep, for Cecily's bold declaration worried her beyond measure.

~

THE NEXT MORNING, Cecily had already arisen by the time Lydia opened her eyes. She looked across at her empty, unmade bed and frowned. It was unusual for her to be up and about so early, and a sense of foreboding crept into Lydia's mind when she remembered the previous night's events.

Did Cecily truly intend to elope with the guard or had it all been bravado in light of the alcohol she had consumed? The fact that she was conspicuous by her absence, confirmed to Lydia that she may have already made up her mind. Lord, she hoped she was wrong.

Sliding her feet from the bed, she hurriedly walked over to the jug of water and pouring some into the bowl, began to wash herself.

Soon she was dressed and her hair neatly pinned for the day ahead. She had given herself just enough time to break her fast in the kitchens before she would be required to tend to the queen's needs, so she swiftly exited the room, hoping to find Cecily already there.

But she was to be disappointed. Cecily was nowhere to be seen. Her one last hope was that she was already tending to the queen, but she had a sick feeling that her hope was going to be in vain.

Her intuition was confirmed when Queen Catherine enquired as to Cecily's whereabouts. "Is she ill? If that is the case, then she has my sympathy, but I will not stand for anyone shirking their duty for no reason." She was sitting in front of her dressing table whilst Lady Frances, another lady-in-waiting, fashioned her hair. "Was she still abed when you left your room?"

Lydia replied carefully, not wishing to get Cecily into trouble. "No. I wonder if she went to the garderobe, Your Majesty. Would you like me to go and see what is delaying her?"

The queen waved her hand in the air. "Yes, I think it is wise. Once you have affirmed all is well, I need you to go to the kitchens and fetch my breakfast. Make haste, I am quite famished this morning."

Lydia curtseyed and quickly left the queen's quarters. Arriving back at her room, she was dismayed to find there was still no sign of Cecily. She clapped a hand over her mouth and sat down on the end of her bed. What could she do, and more importantly, how long could she cover for her?

Cecily had acted without thinking and had put her future in jeopardy. If anyone found out she was with John Russell, her reputation would be sullied, of that there was no doubt. Procuring a suitable husband would be out of the question.

Rising up from the bed, Lydia quickly left the room and ran her errand for the queen, returning with a small tray of food and drink, all cooked to the queen's exacting specifications. She placed it down on one of the small tables near Queen Catherine.

As the queen settled down to partake of her breakfast, she addressed Lydia, "What of Miss Walters? Is she ill? I can send my physician to look at her."

"To be truthful, I know not where she is, Your Majesty." It was all she could say without getting herself into trouble. If she said Cecily was abed, then the physician would quickly confirm Cecily was certainly not in her bed and she would be found out to be a liar. She could only cover for her so far.

The queen paused, mid bite of her pastry. "What do you mean? How can she just disappear?"

Lydia gulped. "I have no idea, Your Majesty. She was there in bed last night, yet this morning, there is no sign of her. It is most unusual."

"This is most alarming. Fetch one of the guards. I will send someone to find her. Something must be wrong."

Lydia walked to the door and asked one of the guards outside to attend the queen. She listened silently while the queen gave him his orders.

When he left, Queen Catherine addressed her, "Fear not,

Miss Robins. We will locate her. I am certain she will have an acceptable explanation for her absence." She fixed her gaze on Lydia, silently assessing her before stating, "You have said nothing about last night."

Lydia lowered her lashes a little. During all the commotion with Cecily's disappearance, her own distress had gone by the wayside. She answered quietly, "Did you hear what was said?"

The queen nodded. "Was there any truth in what you were accused of?" she enquired, watching her steadily.

Lydia raised her eyes to the queen's. "No, most certainly not. Lady Castlemaine simply wished to sully my name and used Lord Danbye to do so. It was most embarrassing and uncalled for."

"She can be extremely outspoken, and once angered, her vitriol can be most unpleasant. At least my husband saw fit to put her in her place. She should never have attended the ball in the first place. You have my sympathy."

Lydia felt the tension leave her body. Thankfully the queen was a charitable woman and perhaps having had her fill of idle gossip, knew when she heard the truth.

"Thank you, Your Majesty."

"Put it behind you and ignore any gossip you may overhear. Most people have nothing better to do, I am afraid, but know that here, in my rooms, I will not tolerate such malice."

It heartened Lydia to have her support and her spirits lifted.

After breakfast had been cleared away, Lydia spent most of the morning learning a new dance with the queen and several other ladies-in-waiting, but she managed to miss most steps because her mind was too involved on other matters. The queen stopped at one point and her tone full of exasperation, asked, "What is the matter with you this morning, Miss Robins? Your head is in the clouds. Have I not told you to forget about the gossip last night?"

Lydia nodded contritely, trying to formulate a smile and failing miserably. "Your pardon, Your Majesty."

The queen pursed her lips and then said astutely, "If you are worried about Miss Walters, there is no need. The guards will locate her."

"Forgive me, Your Majesty, in all truth, I am very concerned."

"As a good companion should be. It does you credit, but please concentrate."

Lydia forced a small smile and resumed the practice. Not only was she worried about Cecily but also wondering when Lord Danbye would make an appearance. What if the queen denied their marriage?

Another half hour later, the queen's guard returned and informed her that he had found no sign of Cecily.

"You have checked the infirmary?" she enquired.

The guard nodded.

"Well, wherever can she have gone? Has she been kidnapped?" the queen exclaimed before turning to Lydia. "When did you last see Miss Walters?"

"Last night when we went to bed, Your Majesty," she reaffirmed, "but since then, nothing. I am perplexed as to where she can be."

She disliked lying to her, but she really didn't want Cecily to get into trouble, and the longer she could delay that, the better. So for now, she would tell no one and hope that Cecily would return to court of her own volition and more to the point, without John Russell.

The queen turned back to the guard. "Take another guard with you and scour not only the palace, but also outside the palace. Find out what has happened. Someone must have seen or heard something. Her parents placed her here in our safe keeping and now she has disappeared. Something is afoot and we must find out what. Now make haste!"

Lydia twisted her hands together in front of her nervously.

Lying to the queen was bad enough, but if she found out Cecily's true intentions, then there would be hell to pay. God's bones. Why did Cecily have to be so impetuous?

The queen approached her and put a hand on her sleeve. "Go to your room and see if you can find a note or some evidence as to where Miss Walters may be. Return if you discover anything."

Lydia curtseyed and quickly headed back to her room, her eyes wide in her face, hoping against hope that Cecily would have returned.

# CHAPTER 8

*L*ydia reached her room in record time and closing the door behind herself, she leaned against the hard wood. By the rood, what a mess she found herself in. She had actually lied to the queen! Needless to say, there was no sign of Cecily.

She worried her bottom lip with her teeth as she pondered on the consequences of withholding the truth and then she silently admonished herself for worrying needlessly. Who was going to tell anyone? Certainly not Cecily. God's bones, she was going to find herself in so much trouble when her parents found out. Did she really love John Russell that much, to jeopardize her relationship with them? It would seem so.

A knock on her door startled her out of her reverie, and swallowing hard, she turned around. "Who is it?" she asked.

"Lord Danbye."

She quickly opened the door to find him standing there, his face full of concern.

"May I come in?" he asked.

"Of course." She stepped aside as he entered and asked him, "I am guessing by your expression that word has reached you of Cecily's disappearance?"

"Yes. Where on earth has she gone? Did she say anything to you?"

Lydia shook her head. "No, not a word." She turned her back on him and indicated her unmade bed. "She was here last night when I returned, but she was gone before I awoke."

"What did she say to you last night?"

"Oh, this and that. Just idle chit chat, really." She turned around to find him staring at her solemnly.

"Are you telling me the truth?" he probed, his eyes searching her face.

She raised her chin indignantly. "Of course, I am!"

"Because if I find out you have been lying to me, then you will reap the consequences, do you understand? This is a very serious matter."

She knew exactly what kind of trouble she'd be in as well. Despite this knowledge, a wave of desire swept through her at the thought of going over his strong thighs. Lydia gulped and tried to act nonchalant. "I am just as worried as everyone else. If I knew where she was, I would say so."

"Even if she told you to keep it secret?"

"Of course!" Lydia nodded emphatically.

"Liar."

Lydia looked at him sharply. "What do you mean by that?"

"I mean, my dearest Lydia, that I know you too well and you are exhibiting signs of lying. I will give you one last chance to tell me the truth, or I will put you straight over my knee."

Lydia's heart started thumping and she took a step backwards. "Honestly, Lord Danbye, I am telling you the truth."

She watched as he shook his head and his eyes fixed on hers. He began to remove his long coat. Throwing it on a nearby chair, Lydia's eyes followed it before flashing back to his. He was in the process of rolling up his sleeves and Lydia knew without a shadow of a doubt that those large hands of his would soon be descending onto her backside.

Nervously, she held up her hand, all the while backing away from him. "Lord Danbye, there is no need for this. I assure you, I am not lying. I am just as worried as you are."

Good lord, this wasn't going well. Her bottom was in for a roasting if she didn't reveal the truth. When his hand snaked out and took hold of her delicate wrist, her decision was made. "Very well! I will tell you," she relented.

He drew her to him and peered down at her hard. "The truth, and nothing but the truth."

At such close proximity and with the threat of a spanking looming, it was hard to concentrate. She gulped and spoke hurriedly. "She has run away with one of the guards. A man named John Russell."

Lord Danbye looked shocked. "A guard? Are you certain of this?"

Lydia nodded. "She is in love with him, and when she found out I would be leaving court to be married, she decided she wanted to do the same."

"God's bones. She has lost her senses."

"What will you do?" she asked him breathlessly. It felt good to share her burden. It was a heavy load to carry on her small shoulders.

He released her and ran a hand over his moustache, whilst he pondered on what to do. "At least we know who she is with now and her intentions. I will send out some guards to track him, visit John's lodgings and his hometown. Chances are, he will have taken her somewhere he knows." He sighed heavily. "What a silly girl."

He turned his attention back to Lydia. "As for you, my dearest Lydia, let this be a warning. I will not tolerate lying on any level. Ever. It is commendable that you revealed the truth but you should have done so straight away. You are lucky I do not give you a sound thrashing for lying in the first place."

She chewed her bottom lip and nodded silently, agreeing. Good lord, those hands of his were huge and she didn't fancy serving the queen whilst having the discomfort of a red-hot bottom.

He placed his hand on her small chin and tilted her face up to his. "If you hear from her, in any way, shape or form, you are to tell me immediately. It is for her own good that this madness is stopped. Her parents need not be informed if we can get her back here before any scandal is publicised." He paused and leaned down to kiss her parted lips. Her heart fluttered at the contact.

"I would have your promise," he said before kissing her again.

She nodded, and raising her arms, she circled his neck as he pulled her closer, his mouth ravishing hers.

Lydia trembled with desire, the passion she felt for him threatening to almost overwhelm her. Finally, Lord Danbye broke off the kiss and, holding her close to his heart, said, "Tell no one what you have told me, not even the queen. Go about your duties as normal."

"When will you speak to the queen about our intention to marry?"

"I think we should wait until we have located Cecily before giving her our news. It may not be well received at the moment."

He gave her one last brief kiss before retrieving his jacket and heading to the door.

"Godspeed, Lord Danbye. I hope you find them before any scandal ensues," Lydia said.

He paused at the door and turned to look at her. "I will return as soon as I can." And with a brief smile, he was gone.

Lydia sat down on the bed and placed her fingertips over her lips, still softly swollen from his passionate kiss. Her nether regions felt warm with a longing that as yet, she had no experience of. What would it feel like to be married to him, to feel his manhood inside her? She had often heard the maids speak of sexual encounters when they had no idea she was listening, but most of it had gone straight over her head. Some things, however, had made her eyes widen and she had a fair idea of what was supposed to happen between a man and a woman.

The idea of doing such things with Lord Danbye excited her beyond belief. She just hoped that this nonsense with Cecily would be sorted out before she left court. An alarming thought came into her mind. What if the queen refused for her to leave her employ and denied her marriage because of Cecily's untimely departure?

Lydia swore softly. If Cecily's actions scuppered her marriage plans, then she would never forgive her. Ever!

LYDIA RETURNED to the queen's rooms a little while later and informed her that she had found nothing to indicate where Cecily could have gone.

"It is such a mystery," exclaimed the queen, looking puzzled. "If she is not found by this evening, we shall have to send word to her parents, but until then I will not burden them with such worrying news."

She hoped for Cecily's sake that Lord Danbye found her before anyone else and that she was still unwed. As to how she would explain her absence to the queen, she knew not but it had better be convincing.

It wasn't until late evening when Lord Danbye returned and thankfully he was not alone. A very dejected looking Cecily accompanied him. Just one look at her face, told Lydia that she had been on the receiving end of Lord Danbye's wrath.

He had taken her straight to her room, where Lydia had already retired for the evening, having been dismissed from her duties. He stood by the window, his arms folded over his broad chest, looking extremely stern.

"Is everything as it should be?" Lydia asked Cecily. "You are yet unwed?"

Cecily nodded and eyed Lord Danbye sullenly. "Yes. We did not even have time to seek out a priest."

"Where is John Russell?" Lydia asked her.

Lord Danbye replied in her stead, "Returned to his post, where he will remain until morning and they will no longer see one another on a personal basis." His eyes shot to Cecily. "Is that not correct, Miss Walters?"

She nodded miserably and then in a small stance of defiance, spat, "It is unfair to keep us apart when we love one another. How would you like it if you were kept from Lydia?"

He immediately strode over and pointed his finger in her face. "You dare to take that tone with me when I have saved you from making a terrible mistake?"

Lydia cringed. Lord Danbye's anger was palpable and just the finger raised in warning should have alerted Cecily to the danger she was in, but she still attempted to put her point across.

"It would never have been a mistake. We are meant to be together," she argued.

"You foolish girl. Your head is in the clouds. What you speak of is just fantasy. I have a good mind to tell the queen exactly what has happened and let her full wrath fall upon your empty head."

Lydia quickly tried to placate him, "Lord Danbye, please take pity on her. Her emotions are understandably high and she is not thinking properly, are you, Cecily?"

Cecily's eyes flashed to hers, and for a moment, Lydia thought she would continue but reason seemed to win and her shoulders slumped a little in defeat. "This is so unfair."

"No, it is not." Lord Danbye argued, "You cannot see it now, but you will. I suggest you take this time to think upon your actions and get a good night's sleep, for in the morning, the queen will have questions that need answering. I will send word to her that you are safely returned and there is no longer any reason to worry." He paused and gave her a hard stare. "The explanation of your disappearance will be down to you."

Cecily gave a disgruntled little humph and then walked over to her bed, leaving Lydia to speak with Lord Danbye. Taking her hand, he drew her over to the door Raising her hand, he kissed the soft skin, sending shivers down her spine..

"I will leave you to talk some sense into her. Good night, my sweet Lydia."

"Good night, Lord Danbye," she whispered.

When he had gone, Lydia locked the door for the night and went and sat down on her bed, opposite Cecily. "I still cannot believe you actually eloped with a guard. What on earth were you thinking?"

Cecily threw her hands up in the air in despair. "I want to be with him, Lydia. As his wife. Lord Danbye should never have interfered."

"What does John have to say about that? He has returned to his duties easily enough."

Cecily's eyes narrowed with anger. "Yes, Lord Danbye threatened to have him dismissed and told him he would not easily find work again once word got out. He is mean!"

"He seeks only to protect you," Lydia assured her. "Imagine the life you would have led, Cecily. Your parents would likely have disowned you. Do you really want that?"

"If it means being with John, then I will gladly sacrifice it."

Lydia pursed her lips. Cecily was more stubborn than she had previously thought. "What are you going to say to Queen Catherine?" she asked. "You cannot tell her you eloped."

"Lord Danbye suggested I tell her that I went to visit a friend who is sick and it took longer than I had anticipated."

"She will be mad with you, but at least it sounds feasible."

Lydia stood up. "It is time I went to sleep. If you are to be fit and well for the morning, then I suggest you do the same. You will need your wits about you when Queen Catherine starts interrogating you."

Cecily sighed heavily but thankfully, she took Lydia's advice and began to undress.

~

THE NEXT MORNING, the queen eyed Cecily sceptically. "A friend? You were absent all day and had everyone worrying about you. I think that is rather reckless, even for you, Miss Walters!"

Lydia's eyes widened. She was mad and rightly so. She would be even madder if she knew the truth. She glanced at Cecily to see she was thankfully looking quite contrite. She had feared she might throw caution to the wind and actually confess what had happened, but luckily, reason seemed to have won.

"I am truly sorry, Your Majesty," Cecily apologised. "Poor Francis was most unwell, and I stayed with her until her mama came. I understand you are disappointed in me." She looked down at the ground and Lydia almost wanted to applaud, for her performance was without fault.

"Yes, I am mightily disappointed. I would be perfectly within my rights to send you packing back to your parents. You would have even more explaining to do then."

Cecily shuffled her feet, keeping her eyes lowered.

There was silence for a moment whilst the queen studied her downturned head and then seeming to come to a decision she pursed her lips and said, "However, I am willing to forgive you just this once. You have served me well so far, and in a way, I commend you." She paused as Cecily raised her head and met her stern gaze. "You have a caring nature and it was most kind of you to remain by your friend's side. A friend in need is a friend indeed, as they say." She adjusted the folds of her skirt before adding, "But it must never happen again. Your duty is to me and before you even think of leaving the grounds, you are to ask my permission beforehand. At least that way, I can ensure your safety. Perhaps even have a guard accompany you."

*Good lord,* thought Lydia, *how close to the truth she was!*

"Now, take that tray down to the kitchens and when you return, you and Miss Robins can sort out my clothes for this afternoon. I wish to visit Saint James' Park. It is beautiful this time of year."

Cecily curtseyed politely and, taking the breakfast tray, quickly left the room. Lydia breathed a sigh of relief and asked the queen which clothing she would prefer to wear for her journey, before also leaving and going to the wardrobe room.

That was a crisis averted, thanks to Lord Danbye. Hopefully the queen would find no objection to her marrying him and all would be well.

LORD DANBYE finally managed to speak with Queen Catherine in the late afternoon when she had returned from her outing. She was taking a walk in the gardens before supper and he chose that time to approach her.

"Your Majesty, may I speak with you?"

She smiled broadly. "Of course, Lord Danbye." She turned to the two women accompanying her and ushered them a little farther away, out of earshot. "Now, what do you wish to speak of?"

He walked next to her, keeping in time with her small paces. "I wish to marry Lydia Robins and would ask your permission to do so."

"You wish to marry Miss Robins? So the rumours may have some truth to them then?" She stopped and looked at him, raising a delicate eyebrow.

He shook his head. "No, Your Majesty. Lydia was just as innocent then as she is now but I have asked her to be my wife and she has accepted—as long as you have no objection." He looked at her expectantly.

"She is a beautiful girl, Lord Danbye, and very conscientious. I will be sad to lose her." She plucked a small flower from a nearby bush and looked down at it. "But like a delicate flower, she attracts attention, and mayhap, it is time for her to leave court. I have enough flowers to contend with."

"Indeed." Lord Danbye nodded his head, understanding her point completely. "Then I can tell her you have given your consent?"

"Yes, and promise me, Lord Danbye, that you will treat her well. If not, I shall hear about it and so will the king," she warned him.

"She has already captured my heart, Your Majesty, and will only receive my full respect. I will make her happy."

She laughed softly. "You are in love, it is clear to see. I give you my blessing. Now go to her and tell her your news."

Lord Danbye didn't need telling twice. He bowed to Queen Catherine and set off in search of his future bride.

LYDIA WAS IN HER ROOM, changing her gown, when Lord Danbye knocked on her door. She told him she wouldn't be a minute whilst hastily fastening the pins on her bodice. Patting herself down, she opened the door.

He smiled at her and before she had time to think, he had placed his hands on her waist and lifted her high up into the air. "The queen has given her permission, Lydia!"

Lydia gasped loudly and flung her hands around his neck as much from excitement as from keeping her balance. "Truly?"

He placed her down on the ground and quickly captured her

lips with his in a searing kiss which left her breathless. "Yes, you shall be mine, Lydia Robins," he declared, his eyes feasting on her delicate beauty. "Speak to the queen later, or tomorrow, and as soon as she allows you to leave her services, we shall return to Barnham."

"I do hope my parents will have no objection," Lydia said worriedly.

"I cannot see they will, but we shall not dwell on that at the moment. I would far rather kiss those sweet lips of yours."

Lydia smiled suggestively and, pressing herself against his large body, drew his head down to hers and kissed him sweetly, her little tongue hurrying to play with his.

As innocent as she was, instinct came to the fore and she wanted to see what effect it would have on him. When his arms tightened around her waist and he gave a low groan, deep in his throat, she knew a great sense of satisfaction. He wanted her.

He broke away and they looked at each other, their hearts beating, their faces flushed with passion. Lifting her hand, he kissed her knuckles. "I desire and love you more than I can tell you, my dearest Lydia. The sooner we are married and I have you safe in my home, the better."

"I am in agreement. The sooner I leave this court and all its intrigue, the safer I shall feel. It has been an experience, but not one I would wish to repeat." He captured her lips once more and she lost herself to his expert touch, her body trembling with excitement at the new life that awaited her.

# CHAPTER 9

Two weeks later, Lydia returned home to her parents. She had already sent word ahead so they knew to expect her, but she had refrained from telling them about her impending marriage.

Lord Danbye had deemed it necessary to ask her father's permission, so for now, as much as she was dying to tell them, it was to be kept a secret.

Her mother came down the steps to greet her wearing a worried expression, instantly asking her if she had somehow misbehaved and been banished from court.

"Mama! Do you think so little of me?" Lydia said, rolling her eyes.

"Of course not, my dear, but you have only been at court for such a short while, what else am I to think."

"Let me come inside and I shall explain." She began to walk up the steps. "Where is Papa?"

"Resting his leg. It aggravates him still but not nearly as much now Doctor Hargreaves has changed his medicine." She followed Lydia into the parlour. "Take a seat and I will order you some refreshments. Then you can tell me the true reason for your early return from court."

Lydia went to say something but her mother held her hand up, stopping her. "And I mean the true reason. I can read you like a book, dearest, and you have a tale to tell!"

Lydia reflected on her words as she swept out of the parlour, realising that keeping a secret from her mother was like climbing the highest mountain—nigh on impossible. She smiled. It felt good to be back home. She had found life at court exciting at first, but that had soon worn off when she realised how conniving people could be.

Her mother returned within minutes, and taking a seat opposite Lydia, she tapped her fingers on the edge of the arm and peered at her intently. "So what have you to tell me?"

For a moment, she thought about lying but then realised it would be pointless. Her mother would find out anyway. She always did. "Well, this may come as a surprise and I hope you have no objection to this, but Lord Danbye wishes to marry me."

Her mother gasped and held a hand to her chest. "Truly?"

Lydia nodded.

"Well, I am quite surprised. Not the fact that he wishes to marry, for obviously a man of his standing would wish to find himself a noteworthy bride. It is the fact that he wishes to marry you and I do not mean that in a condescending way, dearest. Not at all. It is just that you are half his age and dare I say it, a little headstrong."

Lydia pulled a face. "Age does not matter, Mama, and as for being headstrong, well, mayhap that is a good thing. If I am to run his household, then I am certain that will come in useful." She smiled happily. "Besides, he loves me and I love him in return."

Her mother returned her smile. "Yes, I can see you are in love."

"Do you object?"

"No, dearest, not at all. In fact, quite the opposite. I am delighted for you. He is quite a catch and I know you will be well provided for. I admire him greatly, and to think he will become part of our family, is wondrous news."

"I am glad you feel like that; I just hope Papa feels the same. Queen Catherine has given her permission so I cannot see Papa will have any objection."

"No, he will be just as thrilled as I, my dear." The door opened and the maid appeared with a tray of drinks and pastries. "Set it down on the table, Agatha."

When she had gone, Lydia's mother poured the coffee, and smiling, she handed a cup to Lydia, saying, "And you are of a mind to obey your new husband?" She teased her gently.

"Of course."

"You must love him to be so biddable."

"I can be biddable when I wish to be," Lydia replied, arching an eyebrow, "but I am no weakling."

"Yes, you can be very strong willed. I just hope our Lord Danbye knows what he is taking on."

Lydia looked at her sharply, ready to defend herself but saw her mother's eyes twinkle with mirth. She laughed in response and took a bite of a pastry. Oh yes, Lord Danbye knew exactly how mischievous she could be—hadn't she been spanked enough for it already? But that was part of her attraction to him—the fact that he was stern enough to take her in hand when needed. He would make a good husband and now that she had been to court, she realised more than ever how rare a thing that was.

Her mother interrupted her thoughts. "How goes Cecily? Was she sorry to see you leave?"

"Yes, she threatened to leave as well at first, but we had a little talk, and she decided to stay." Lydia refrained from revealing Cecily's dalliance with John Russell. That would, and should, remain in the past.

"How did you find working alongside her? I do not sense the

same animosity from you that I felt before you left. You were quite hostile, dearest."

Lydia shrugged. "Well, she can be so annoying. Always prattling on. Why use one word when ten will do?" She rolled her eyes. "But in all honesty, having her dominate the conversation gave me time to observe people, which was very interesting. Lady Castlemaine proved to be very conniving and was even asked to leave court by the king himself."

"My goodness!" exclaimed her mother. "What did she do to incur his wrath?"

Lydia began to inform her mother of all the goings on at court. By the time she had finished, her mother's mouth was practically hanging open.

"Goodness me, Lydia. All this happened in but a few months. I declare, I am relieved that you are home and even more so that Lord Danbye will be looking after you. As I have said before, trouble does seem to follow you around, and marriage to such a good man will surely keep you safe from anything happening like this in the future. So yes, you most definitely have my blessing."

She leaned back in her chair and took a sip of her coffee, her mind deep in thought as she digested Lydia's revelations. Lydia was silently pondering her mother's words. Yes, marriage to Lord Danbye would keep her safe from court life but would she be able to behave enough to keep herself safe from those disciplinary hands of his? Only time would tell.

Two weeks later, Lydia became Lady Danbye. As her mother had predicted, Lydia's father had no objection whatsoever to their marriage and had given his consent immediately. He admired Lord Danbye greatly, and to have his daughter marry such an esteemed man, gave him a sense of pride.

So, after a simple ceremony and a small reception at her parents' house, Lydia found herself on her way to her new home, Seven Oaks.

"Are you happy, Lydia?" Lord Danbye asked her. She was seated next to him in their carriage and they were quite alone.

"Very happy, my lord. And you?"

"Need you ask? I have just married the most beautiful woman in the whole of Christendom."

Lydia blushed at the compliment and he gently ran a finger down her cheek. "And you blush so becomingly, my dear." The carriage juddered to a halt and Lord Danbye looked out of the window. "Ah, here we are."

Lydia looked past him to see the house all lit up with lanterns. Her new home. She had already met the staff and they had been most respectful.

Percy, the steward, opened the carriage door for them. "Good evening, my lord, lady."

"Evening, Percy," Lord Danbye replied, his deep tones filling the air. "Is the master suite ready?"

The newly built east wing was where they would spend most of their time, and Lord Danbye had spared no expense for his new bride in fitting out their bedroom so that she would have every comfort.

Percy replied proudly, "Of course, my lord, as you instructed."

"Excellent." Lord Danbye stepped out of the carriage and immediately turned around to assist Lydia. She put her small hand in his and stepped down onto the driveway. She couldn't help but feel a little nervous about the impending night and how it would be. Would Lord Danbye prove to be a good lover? How would she know? Would it hurt?

Lydia had tried asking her mother only a few days earlier about what would occur on her wedding night, but it had all been a little embarrassing. The main advice she offered was to obey her husband and allow him to take command, and to run a respectable household. Oh, and to be well-behaved and demure.

Lydia's nose crinkled up at the thought of being well-behaved. Did that mean boring? Having no opinion? Ha! If Lord Danbye did something she disagreed with, she would certainly tell him. In her opinion, that was something he would have to deal with. Her stubborn nature would make sure of it.

As for the actual sexual act itself, well, her mother wasn't very forthcoming. Lydia could tell she was extremely uncomfortable talking about it but had pressed her for advice. So realising Lydia wasn't going to give up, she had told her to expect a little pain the first time, but, afterwards, her body would adjust and that all a husband expected from a wife was to do her duty as and when he wished.

She hadn't gone into any true details, so Lydia had not pried any further.

So here she was, on the threshold of womanhood, without a clue of what it entailed. So, yes, she was nervous.

IT DIDN'T TAKE LONG to find themselves alone, Percy having discreetly disappeared back downstairs. Taking Lydia in his arms, Lord Danbye tipped her face up so that their eyes met. His open look of passion almost took her breath away.

"Finally, we are alone." He brushed a strand of hair away from her eyes. "You are so beautiful… and you are mine."

Lydia blushed becomingly as she lost herself in his deep brown eyes.

"Do not be afraid," he murmured softly. "I will treat you gently, my sweet Lydia."

When he touched his firm mouth against hers, Lydia felt a warmth suffuse her whole body before his lips fully captured hers, and kissing her soundly, he moulded her body against his.

Lydia's stomach fluttered with excitement and she trembled slightly, placing her small hands on his broad shoulders, her slim fingers running over his muscular form.

He pulled away briefly, to nuzzle her neck, his hot breath making her dizzy with desire. "Come, I shall help you undress."

His voice brooked no argument and before long, she found herself naked to his admiring gaze. She had wondered what this moment would feel like. Would she feel self-conscious or embarrassed? But, no. His love for her was plain to see and it only made her feel a sense of wonder and anticipation.

"You are simply beautiful, Lydia." Scooping her up in his arms, he laid her on the bed. Without taking his eyes off her, he quickly divested himself of his clothing before joining her, his strong arms wrapping around her slender frame and his lips, once again, claiming her own.

His tongue sought entrance, entwining with her own and leaving her breathless with desire. She felt his hand cup her bottom, kneading the flesh gently, his kiss deepening.

He then moved a trail down her body, kissing and teasing until he reached her womanhood. Lydia parted her thighs naturally and gasped with joy when she felt his hot tongue sear her feminine core.

"My lord, 'tis heavenly!"

His large hands held her buttocks while his tongue skilfully brought her to orgasm. She arched her back when it ripped through her, her small cries filling the night air. Lord Danbye quickly moved up her body, his lips meshing with hers and then she felt him at her entrance, his hair roughened thighs covering her own. She stiffened, a little frightened as to how it would feel but trusting him completely.

~

LORD DANBYE PUSHED into her slowly, not wanting to hurt her but knowing her first time would be painful. Her tight sheath stretched around him and upon reaching her maidenly barrier, he stopped for a moment, to let her adjust to his size. It was sheer torture and a reflection of his self-control.

She clutched his arms tightly but made no move to stop him. His kiss deepened, and with one quick thrust, he broke through the thin barrier and she was his. She whimpered, her small cry fluttering softly against his lips.

"I am sorry, my love," he said as he raised his head so he could see her eyes. "But the worst is over. From now, you will feel only pleasure." His lips covered hers and slowly, he began to thrust into her, his hips moving in a steady rhythm that soon had her moaning softly into his mouth.

He felt her body tighten and knew she was nearing climax, her cries increasing in intensity. He broke the kiss and moved lower to cover one rosy nipple with his mouth, laving his tongue over the sensitive peak until she gasped his name, her orgasm rippling through her slim body. Her cries of wonder heartened him, and knowing he had given her satisfaction, he began to bring himself to completion, pumping his thick weapon into her soft, welcoming body. His orgasm, when it came, made him cry out with its intensity, gripping her hips tightly as a wave of pleasure washed over him.

He collapsed over her, mindful of his weight, and looked into her face. Her cheeks were flushed and her eyes sparkled happily. She placed her hand on his cheek and then slipped it around his neck, bringing his face down so she could kiss him softly.

He rolled onto his side, bringing her pliable form with him, his cock still buried in her warm sheath. "I am sorry for hurting you, my love," he breathed. "But now your maidenhead has been removed, next time you will feel only pleasure."

She idly stroked his back. "It hurt only a little—but afterwards it was truly wonderful!"

Her words stirred him and he grew hard again. Her eyes widened when she felt it. "My lord!"

Smiling wickedly, he grabbed her bottom and, rolling onto his back, drew her up so she was riding him. He feasted on her ripe breasts free of their restrictive clothing. She was perfect in every way. Placing his hands on her hips, he began to thrust into her lush body, relishing her cries of ecstasy as he took her to new heights, where this time she would experience only pleasure.

FOR THE NEXT TWO WEEKS, they could not seem to get enough of one another. Lord Danbye had taught her so much in the ways of love. Not only her own body and responses, but how to pleasure him as well. Her love and respect for him seemed to grow every day that passed and by the look in his eyes, she knew it was reciprocated.

Her husband owned several horses and had given her a mare called Plume. She was dark grey and very placid. The fact that she was so amenable, was perfect for Lydia, having only ridden once or twice in her life. To be truthful, she was usually a little wary of horses but Plume had such a sweet nature that she soon fell in love with her.

Seven Oaks' grounds were vast and it was lovely just to sedately walk around the fields on Plume's back, enjoying the fresh air whilst Lord Danbye concentrated on work he had to sort out or the overseeing of his property.

It was early afternoon and she was sitting side-saddle on Plume, walking sedately alongside the stream when movement caught her eye to her right. She looked up to find Lord Danbye trotting towards her. His horse was much bigger and more powerful than little Plume, a black horse named Titan and just as beautiful. Although she would never want to ride him. She knew her limits.

She smiled easily when Lord Danbye caught up to her. "Dearest Lydia. I thought I would join you."

"Have you finished your work?"

Lord Danbye nodded. "Yes. I also found I could hardly concentrate as thoughts of you kept entering my mind."

His eyes sparkled with desire and Lydia immediately felt her nether regions grow damp with want. "Shall we ride back to the house?" she asked, her voice a little breathless.

"Nay, we shall remain here."

Lydia's face fell and Lord Danbye immediately let out a low chuckle. "We have no need to go to the house. I intend to make love to you right here, right now."

"Here?" Lydia gasped, her teeth biting on her lower lip. "But what if someone comes along?"

"They will not. We are quite safe, I assure you."

He dismounted and tied Titan to a low tree branch, before turning to help Lydia dismount and securing Plume to another branch.

Taking her hand, he led her over to a fallen log, and before she realised what was happening, he had pulled her straight down over his lap.

"My lord, what do you do?" she protested, trying to rise, but he kept her firmly held down with one thickly muscled arm. "I have not been bad," she breathed in alarm. "I thought you were going to make love to me?"

His deep voice reached her ears and she shivered expectantly. "Yes, I am but I wish to show you another side of spanking. Another side of pain."

Lydia closed her eyes, not certain whether to fight him or accept what he intended. What did he mean? Another side of pain? Leaving her trust in him, she sighed with longing when she felt his hands begin to lift her skirts. His touch was electric.

He ran a hand over her buttocks, caressing the silky skin and sending tremors of excitement through Lydia's slender frame.

Suddenly, she felt a stinging smack on her buttocks, and then another, and another. She emitted a low gasp, not certain whether she liked it or not, but his hand continued to pepper her bottom lightly until she felt a warm glow on both cheeks. Just as she thought she could take no more, he moved his hand lower and, slipping a finger into her tight sheath, brought her swiftly to orgasm.

"Oh, my lord!" she panted, still lying over his lap, too sated to move.

"Now you know, my sweet Lydia, that there are many ways of reaching fulfilment." He turned her over, lifting her up in his arms. Walking her over to the grass, he laid her down. Lowering his britches, she watched in fascination as he revealed his engorged manhood. He too was obviously as aroused as she was.

Within seconds, he had raised her skirts and lifted her legs. His thick weapon entered her willing body. Lydia cared not a jot if anyone saw them. She was so aroused that nothing would have stopped their union come hell or high water.

She placed her hands on his hips, encouraging his every stroke until with a guttural cry, they reached their pinnacle together, united as one.

For a moment, Lord Danbye collapsed over Lydia, mindful of his weight but too spent to move off her just yet. Lydia breathed in his masculine scent, savouring the close proximity and realising that she was so lucky to have found such a wonderful partner in life.

Raising his head, Lord Danbye looked down at her and smiled, his eyes full of love. "You have made a wonderful wife, Lydia. I am blessed."

"As am I, my lord, as am I."

~

A FEW DAYS LATER, Lord Danbye was called away to court and Lydia found herself on her own. He had promised to return as soon as he could, but who knew when that would be. She just hoped it was days instead of weeks. So for now, Lydia was left to her own devices.

The weather was beautiful, so she had taken a blanket and was sitting with her back propped against a big oak tree, reading one of the books from Lord Danbye's rather impressive library. Flicking over a page, she absently swiped an insect away from the page as her hungry mind devoured the story. She had always loved reading, and to know she had such a vast array of books at her fingertips, was wonderful.

Suddenly, she became aware of a hissing noise. At first she thought she was imagining it but, no, there it was again. She looked up and listened intently, trying to work out where it was coming from.

"*Psst!*"

Lydia's heart began to race. Who the devil was it? Then all of a sudden, a head popped up, just above the nearby shrubbery, almost giving her a heart attack.

"Cecily!" Lydia gasped, breathing a huge sigh of relief. For a moment, she had thought it was someone untoward. One hears such stories. She placed her book down on the grass and quickly stood up, making her way to the bush. "Cecily, what do you do here? Why are you hiding?"

"Lydia, I am in grave trouble!"

Lydia's eyes widened when she heard the fear in Cecily's voice. "What have you done?"

"Is Lord Danbye here? I do not want him to know." Her voice wavered and Lydia quickly told her that he was at court.

"How did you get here? By carriage?" Lydia asked, noting the state of her. Her clothes were quite grimy and her hair a little unkempt where strands were breaking free from the pins.

Cecily shook her head. "By foot. I have been walking for two days. I am so weary." She closed her eyes momentarily.

"Goodness, Cecily, you simply must come inside the house and rest, then we can talk. If I may say, you look rather peaky."

Cecily had never looked so scared. She reached out and touched Lydia's sleeve. "Can you get me indoors without the servants seeing? I would rather they did not know I was here."

Lydia thought hard. "Of course, allow me a few moments to order some tea and it will give us time to get you inside whilst Percy arranges things in the kitchen. Wait here."

Lydia rapidly walked across the lawns and entered inside the house, quickly locating Percy to order some tea and refreshments, telling him she would take it in the parlour.

She waited for him to disappear through the double doors to the kitchens before quickly heading back to her friend.

"Make haste. I will hide you in the parlour. Quickly now!"

The two of them darted to the house in record time, and scooting through the parlour doorway, Lydia secreted Cecily away behind one of the big sofas, completely out of view.

Cecily went to speak but Lydia hushed her to silence, knowing that Percy wouldn't be long in making his appearance. Her mind was doing overtime, wondering what on earth Cecily had done to get herself in trouble, but she would only find out when they were alone.

A few moments later, there was a discreet knock on the door, before Percy entered holding a tray with a pot of tea and some small pastries.

"Shall I put it on the table, my lady?"

"Yes, thank you, Percy."

She waited impatiently whilst he slowly placed the tray as she wished. "Shall I pour?" he asked, raising his eyebrows.

"Oh no, thank you. That will be all." Lydia was trying her best to act nonchalant but in all truth, she was gagging to talk to Cecily.

As soon as the door closed behind him, she rushed over to Cecily. "It is safe now, he has gone."

Cecily stood up and rubbed her forehead. "Goodness, I do not feel at all well."

Lydia studied her intently, noting her pallor and the circles beneath her eyes. Gently, she took her arm and led her over to the seat she had just vacated. Without a word, she filled a cup with the hot tea and added some honey, placing it in front of Cecily. "Drink some of this."

Cecily tentatively took a few sips before sighing heavily, leaning back and closing her eyes, then dragging a hand over her forehead. "Lydia, I am in so much trouble, and I had no one else to turn to."

Lydia placed a hand over one of hers. "Whatever is it, Cecily?"

Cecily leaned forward and placed her head in her hands. "I am with child."

Lydia couldn't help the loud gasp that left her lips. Whatever she had thought she would tell her—it wasn't this. Swallowing hard, she asked her if she was certain.

"Yes."

"I have to ask, but is it John Russell's?"

"Yes." At this point, Cecily started sobbing. Lydia sat down on the chair next to her with a thump and just stared at her, so shocked that she just didn't know how to answer or what to do.

Her mind raced with answers. She couldn't tell Lord Danbye. Hadn't he told Cecily to stop seeing John Russell in the first place? She couldn't tell either of their parents. Lord. Both would be mortified, and more to the point, would they disown Cecily? What a mess.

"Does John Russell know?" Lydia finally managed to ask.

"Yes, and before you ask, he does want to marry me but he is not the man I thought him to be. He has a nasty temper, Lydia. I cannot marry a man like that or bring children into the world with a father like him."

Lydia stared hard at her. "But, Cecily, you surrendered your virginity to him. What were you thinking?"

"It was only once and he said it would be fine."

Lydia snorted. "Yes, he would. He is not the one who has to suffer the consequences." She closed her eyes and rubbed her temples. "I just do not know what to do or say."

She stood up and paced in front of the fireplace, her mind still awhirl. She stopped and looked down at Cecily's bowed head. "Why did you go back to him? Lord Danbye helped you out of one terrible situation and yet you went back for more? What you have done is reckless beyond belief."

"I loved him, Lydia. Even though I knew it was wrong, I just could not resist him."

"It was foolhardy, Cecily."

"Yes, I realise that now in so many ways." She raised her tear-stained face to Lydia and asked, "Can I stay here? At least for now, until I figure out what to do."

"If you stay here, Lord Danbye will find out. I cannot hide you, Cecily." She watched as Cecily's face fell so she quickly added, "Well, maybe for a little while, but not forever. You will have to face up to the consequences sooner or later." She stood up and paced the woven rug. "Maybe if I tell him, he can help you."

"No!" Cecily raised her voice. "He was livid before when he found out I had run away with John, I hate to think what he would say now." She leaned forward, her eyes angry. "And I will not marry John Russell. I cannot, and no one is going to force me."

"Do you know how many months you are into your confinement?"

"It is early, about six or seven weeks, I think." She looked down at her stomach. "I cannot believe there is a child in there. Life is so unfair. It was just the one dalliance and this had to happen. Oh lord, what am I going to do?"

Lydia thought hard. "Well, until we decide what to do, then you must stay here. The left wing is unoccupied. So as long as you remain quiet, you can live there for a little while until we both figure out what we can do. I will bring food and drink." She frowned as a thought occurred to her. "Does the queen know where you have gone?"

"I told her that mother was ill and I had to leave to see her. She is expecting me to return at some point."

Lydia shook her head. "This is a right mess, Cecily. But one way or another, we will figure something out. Now drink the rest of that tea and I will smuggle you up to the west wing."

"I cannot thank you enough, Lydia. I did not know where else to turn."

Lydia laid a hand on her shoulder, hearing the sincerity in her voice. "Fear not, Cecily. We will get through this, one way or another."

She just hoped Lord Danbye never found out what she was doing because as sure as eggs were eggs, it would be her backside that would pay.

## CHAPTER 10

*C*ecily had been at Seven Oaks for three days, and neither she nor Lydia were any closer to a solution to their problem. Try as they might, they just couldn't see a clear path.

Taking a tray of breakfast up the winding back staircase, Lydia knocked on Cecily's door before entering. She was still in bed, so she placed the tray on the table and walked over to the windows, pushing the wooden shutters open to let the light in.

The sunlight filtered across the room and she heard a low moan fill the air. Looking over her shoulder, she noted Cecily had pulled the covers up over her eyes to block out the bright rays. Lydia sent her a smile of commiseration and tried to be upbeat. "How are you feeling, Cecily?"

Cecily tentatively lowered the edge of the sheet and peeped above it. "Awful. Just awful."

Lydia sat down on the edge of the bed and placed the back of her hand over her brow. "You still feel a little hot to me. Something is not right with you, Cecily. I truly think we should send for a midwife. If we speak to Agnes, she could maybe suggest someone—"

She didn't get to finish her sentence before Cecily was

arguing back. "No! I will not see anyone. I do not want anyone to know. I must figure this out by myself."

Lydia stood up, starting to get angry. "How? How can you possibly sort this mess out on your own? You are with child! It is not simply going to go away. For goodness sake, Cecily, be reasonable."

Cecily's lower lip began to tremble and Lydia immediately felt like a heel. Sitting back down on the bed, she placed her arms around her. "Forgive me. I did not mean to be harsh. I am just frustrated at this whole situation."

Lydia comforted her whilst she cried softly. It was all very well hiding at Seven Oaks, but sooner or later, she would have to leave. The situation couldn't go on as it was. She had tried offering to speak to Agnes, their amiable middle-aged cook, a couple of times but Cecily would have none of it. Agnes would surely know someone in the village or nearby who could at least come and examine Cecily without tittle tattling. With enough coin, you could buy any silence.

Suddenly, she became aware of noises outside. Her eyes widened and her heart leapt as she realised what it was—a horse's hooves. Jumping up off the bed, she ran over to the window and looked down.

"God's bones! Lord Danbye has returned. I thought he would be away longer than this. By the rood, what are we going to do?" She spun around, her skirts making a draft as the material settled against her slender legs.

Cecily was staring at her, her eyes wide with fear. "Please do not tell him I am here. Please, Lydia. I beg of you!"

Lydia nibbled on a thumbnail and frantically tried to calm herself. "I must take a deep breath," she muttered aloud. "He will not find out. He cannot!"

Her eyes shot to the breakfast tray. "There is enough food there to last you until this evening." She began clearing the food from the tray onto the little table. "I will take the tray back to my rooms so Percy does not become suspicious." She clutched the tray against her bosom and stared hard at Cecily. "All I ask is that you remain as quiet as a mouse. I will come back tonight when Lord Danbye is asleep, or earlier if I get the chance."

"Thank you, Lydia. I do not know what I would do without you."

With one last look, Lydia swept out of the room and disappeared back down the staircase, quickly making her way across the halls and corridors until she was in the parlour. She just had time to place her tray on the table and put her breakfast utensils back on, before Lord Danbye entered the room.

"Sweetheart!" His deep tones filled the room, instantly sending shivers of desire up her spine. Lord, he was so handsome.

She immediately found herself pulled against his masculine strength as his large arms encircled her slender body.

"I have missed you so!" he declared, pulling away slightly to claim her lips with his own.

She surrendered, blissfully, all thoughts of Cecily flying from her mind while her senses were bombarded with hinted sexual delights from her wonderful husband. He pulled away after kissing her soundly and looked deep into her eyes. "Let me look at you. It has only been a few days, yet it feels like months."

Lydia smiled softly. "I have missed you too, my lord."

"I am glad to hear it." He studied her face intently. "You look very flushed, my dear. Is it just my kiss that did that or do you hide something?" he teased.

It took all of Lydia's willpower to remain calm. "It is just the excitement of seeing you, my lord. 'Tis all."

"Then I am glad for it." His lips claimed her own and she melted into his arms once again. He broke away, murmuring against her lips, "I am not certain I can wait for tonight."

"Then why should we?" Lydia breathed, taking his lower lip between her small white teeth and nipping gently.

She heard his sharp intake of breath, and before she knew what was happening, he had swept her up in his arms and was heading out of the parlour and up the wide staircase. Lydia held on to his broad shoulders and buried her face in his chest. Heavens knew what Percy would say if he saw them!

Reaching their bedroom, Lord Danbye kicked the door open with his booted foot and strode in. Laying his precious cargo down on the bed, he quickly returned to bolt the door, at the same time unbuttoning his britches. Lydia's eyes sparkled with desire, her body alive with the need to feel him inside her. When he turned back to her, his arousal was evident and emboldened by desire, Lydia placed her hand around his engorged manhood, enjoying the feeling of empowerment.

Lord Danbye closed his eyes for a moment and groaned. Within moments, he had Lydia bent over the bed, her skirts over her back and her petticoats pushed aside. She was already wet with desire and when he pushed his manhood inside her soft folds, she almost screamed aloud.

The feeling was bliss. Lord Danbye knew exactly how to please her, and it wasn't long before she was lost to him. His large, masculine hands kneaded her bottom as he thrust into her, again and again, his manhood leaving her breathless with want.

She cried out as she reached her pinnacle at the same time that she felt Lord Danbye stiffen as he released himself inside her.

Satiated, they both fell sideways onto the bed, still joined, his body spooning hers. When her breathing returned to normal, Lydia lazily trailed a hand down his thigh behind her. "That was heavenly, my lord."

Lord Danbye turned her to face him. "Yes, I second that, my love." His lips captured hers, and once again, she felt his manhood harden within her womanly core. Before long, she was lost to his expert touch.

~

*LATE AFTERNOON...*

Lord Danbye had left Lydia to her own devices after lunch because he had some work to discuss with Harrison, one of the farmers who rented his land. It was an ideal time for Lydia to go see Cecily. She had managed to conceal a small roll, a slice of cheese and an apple from lunch to take to her. It wasn't much but it would have to do until supper. Although goodness only knew what she was going to take her then. But she would worry about that later. She would take this one step at a time and worry only when she had to.

Walking across the large entrance hall, she was just about to put her foot on the first stair when there was a loud knock against the front door. She paused and was just wondering whether to answer it herself when Percy appeared out of nowhere. Lydia waited to see who it was and then wished she hadn't. It was Cecily's parents!

There was no way she could disappear into the shadows, as they had already spotted her. So quickly putting down her napkin containing the food for Cecily, she plastered a welcoming smile on her face, and calming her nerves, she walked forward to greet them.

"Good day, Lord and Lady Walters. This is an unexpected pleasure."

"Good day, Lady Danbye. I fear this is not a leisurely visit. We have come to ask for your help. Is Lord Danbye here?" Lord Walters asked, his voice solemn.

Lydia looked at Percy. "Would you fetch Lord Danbye? I think you will find him in his study."

"Indeed, my lady."

Lydia held her hand out towards the parlour. "Would you like to follow me?"

She opened the door across the hallway and Lady Walters sailed into the room, a handkerchief dabbing at her eyes and her husband solemnly walking behind. Before the door had time to close, Lord Danbye appeared, giving Lydia hardly any time to compose herself. She could feel her hands trembling and quickly clasped them together in front of her.

"Lord and Lady Walters. I understand we can mayhap assist you with something?" Lord Danbye closed the door behind him and motioned for them to take a seat. Lydia did the same, seating herself opposite.

Lydia regarded them silently, knowing full well why they were there but doing her best to look as though she didn't have a clue.

Lady Walters was the first to speak. "Lord Danbye, I have come to ask if you have any knowledge of my daughter's whereabouts? Cecily has been missing for nearly a week, and to be truthful, we are worried beyond reason." She sniffled into her hanky and turned tear filled eyes to Lydia. "Perhaps she has been in contact with you, my dear?"

Lydia shifted uncomfortably before replying, "Um, no, she has not. I thought she was still at court. May I ask what happened?" Lydia asked, hoping she sounded sincere. Good lord, she was glad she wasn't on the stage. Her acting skills weren't exactly her forté.

"She left court about six days ago and no one has heard from her since," Lord Walters explained. "There was no reason for her to leave. She even lied to the queen and told her that my wife was ill. Why would she lie? Why would she leave the queen's employ like this? It makes no sense."

"We only knew of her absence when we received a message from Queen Catherine, asking about my health and when Cecily would be returning. Of course, we were worried sick. At first we thought mayhap she had intended to come home and she might have encountered some trouble on her way back home, but that does not account for her lying to the queen," Lady Walters added, "No. It would seem she had every intention of running away but we know not why." She looked at Lydia again. "She said nothing to you?"

Lydia swallowed hard. "Nay, not a word."

"It is not her usual behaviour. She is usually such a good girl. 'Tis why I think something terrible may have happened to her." Her voice broke on a sob and it took all of Lydia's willpower not to reveal their daughter's whereabouts.

She darted a glance at her husband quickly and then froze, wishing she hadn't. He was staring hard at her and she knew that he knew she was covering for something. She quickly looked away but tried her best to show an outward appearance of calm. Inside, she was in turmoil. She clenched her buttocks, knowing that she would be on the receiving end of a sound spanking if she didn't somehow manage to wriggle her way out of telling him the truth.

But that look of his spoke volumes.

She was going to have to come up with a brilliant lie, but what the hell could she say?

Lord Danbye ascertained within the first few minutes of Lord and Lady Walters visit that somehow, his wife was linked to Cecily's disappearance. He knew the tell-tale signs of lying and his wife was exhibiting many of them. His jaw tightened with anger. She should know better than to lie to him.

But he wouldn't embarrass her in front of their guests. No, he would interrogate her thoroughly when they had gone. And by hook or by crook, she was going to reveal everything she knew and woe betide her if she had done something untoward! Heaven knew what debacle Cecily had gotten herself involved with now.

"Lord and Lady Walters, if I am able to help in any way, please let me know," Lord Danbye said. "I have men on the estate whom I will send out to search for her. I also have many acquaintances at court. Please do not worry, we will find her. I am certain there will be a simple explanation."

Lord Walters stood up and helped his wife to stand by his side. "Thank you for the offer of help, Lord Danbye, 'tis most appreciated. Someone, somewhere, must know where she is."

"Indeed. I shall start the investigations straight away and inform you when I hear anything. Anything at all."

Lord Danbye rang for Percy and he showed them out of the house. As the door closed behind them in the parlour, silence ensued. He watched his wife shift nervously and fiddle with her fingers. Yes, she was hiding something all right.

She stood up and made for the door. "Lydia, come to me."

Her eyes locked with his and despite doing her best to act nonchalant, he could see the fear within their blue depths. "I have an errand to run. I—"

"Whatever it is can wait." He held out his hand. "Come here."

She hesitated for a moment before doing as he bid. When she reached him, she avoided his gaze, keeping her lashes lowered.

He placed a finger on her chin and tilted her small face up to his. "What are you keeping from me, my love?"

Her eyes immediately flashed to his. "Nothing, my lord. What makes you think otherwise?"

He could hear the tell-tale shortness of breath and, placing a hand lightly against her chest, could feel her heart racing beneath his fingertips. "I will ask again, what do you hide?"

His eyes bored into hers and, once again, she lowered her lashes before replying quietly, "Nothing. Nothing at all. I am just as worried as you are about Cecily. Why do you think I know anything?"

"Because I know you, my sweet Lydia."

Lydia was beginning to get angry. He could tell by the way

her eyes flashed and the thinning of her lips. She tried to pull away, but he had a firm grip on her arm. He raised his finger and pointed it in her face. "No, you are not going anywhere except over my knees... unless you reveal the truth."

"Fie, I know nothing!"

Lord Danbye shook his head. "Very well."

He contained her struggling form easily and, lifting her feet off the floor, manhandled her over to one of the chairs. Taking a seat, he drew her straight down over his lap. She tried to scramble straight off, but already used to her ways, he simply threw one of his long legs over hers and she was captured.

"Unhand me! This is unfair!" she hissed angrily.

"Nay, my sweet Lydia. I have told you before that I detest lying. You have chosen to keep this innocent pretence up so I am going to punish you until you tell me the truth." He threw her skirts over her back, exposing her bare bottom.

He felt her whole body stiffen, and she quickly protested, "Nay, my lord. I will not submit!" She flung one of her hands over her bottom, trying her best to protect it.

"Then tell me the truth. That is all you have to do."

"I have told you; I know nothing."

"Very well. Remove your hand."

"Nay, I will not," she spat angrily.

"You are too stubborn for words!" He quickly captured her hand and pinned it to the small of her back, then his other hand came swinging down straight onto both her rounded buttocks. She gasped and bucked, but he wasn't going to release her until her bottom had been thoroughly punished. He set up a steady rhythm, his hand swinging down onto alternate cheeks. She wailed and kicked but he had no intention of stopping until he was good and ready.

*Smack! Smack! Smack!*

"Ow! Please stop, it hurts!" she cried.

"Good!"

After several more heavy swats, he released her hand and pulled her up to stand in front of him. He was satisfied to see her face screwed up, showing her discomfort as she rubbed her bottom.

"So shall I continue, or are you going to tell me what you know?"

～

LYDIA'S BOTTOM was on fire. She should have known not to try to fool him. God, his hands were hard. She rubbed furiously at her backside to alleviate the pain and stared at him sullenly.

"I suggest you take that look off your face unless you want some more," Lord Danbye warned her, raising an eyebrow.

She quickly looked away.

"Well?" he demanded.

Lydia looked down at her feet, stalling for time whilst she tried in vain to think of something to tell him other than the truth. But in all honesty, she had nothing. "She is in the west wing," she blurted, finally revealing Cecily's whereabouts.

He muttered an oath before demanding, "Why the devil are you hiding her? And more to the point, why did you not tell me?"

He stood up and ran a hand through his long hair, clearly vexed but awaiting her explanation. She hesitated, and he began to lose patience. "Well?"

"I chose not to tell you because I did not want you to tell her parents. She is in trouble and needs my help." She looked warily at him. "When you find out the truth, you will throw her out."

"You think that little of me?"

"No, of course not, but her predicament is such that your moral obligation will be to hand her over to her parents. And if you do, I shall never talk to you again!"

He narrowed his eyes for a moment, deep in thought, and

then declared, "Your words leave me only one conclusion—she is with child. Am I correct?"

Lydia nodded miserably and placed her hands over her face. She hated the position Cecily had put her in but at the same time, what else could she have done?

"Lydia, Lydia. Why do you get yourself involved in matters like this?"

She lowered her hands and replied honestly, "She was desperate and I truly had little choice but to help her."

"You should have sent me a message straight away. We should keep no secrets from each other, do you understand?"

He walked over to her and tilted her chin so she had no choice but to look at him. "I hope you learn from this." He ran his thumb over her soft lips, caressing the sensitive skin. "Now, take me to her and we will somehow resolve this problem, one way or another."

CECILY WAS LYING on her side when they entered the room, her body curled up in a foetal position beneath the covers. She looked to be in pain and Lydia immediately rushed to her side.

"Cecily?" She opened her eyes and Lydia could clearly see the distress reflected in them. "What has happened?"

"I am bleeding and my stomach hurts so much," she whispered. "I am scared, Lydia." Her eyes darted to Lord Danbye, noticing him standing in the doorway, and she groaned and closed her eyes. "God's bones!"

Lord Danbye shook his head as he took in the situation. "I am sending for the village midwife."

Neither Lydia nor Cecily made any move to protest, perhaps both realising they had reached the point of no return. Something was clearly wrong and Cecily needed medical intervention.

Lydia held Cecily's hand and watched her husband leave the room. She was glad for his strength. She shifted a little when she remembered that strength had just given her a good bottom warming, but mayhap she had deserved it. She had been reckless and perhaps should have told him the truth from the onset.

She just hoped the midwife would be able to help her friend. She gently stroked Cecily's forehead, trying to give her some comfort whilst they waited.

~

LORD DANBYE STARED out of the parlour window whilst the midwife attended Cecily. Lydia had already been dismissed from the room—the midwife having declared it was no place for a young married woman to be. So she was sitting quietly across the room from her husband, impatiently wondering what was going on.

Before long, there was a tentative knock on the door and Lord Danbye called out, "Come."

The midwife entered the room and he immediately asked how Cecily fared.

"She is settled. I am afraid she has lost the baby but she is young and healthy and will be able to have more. I think, under the circumstances, perhaps this is the best outcome."

"Indeed, it is," Lord Danbye reasoned. "How long should she stay abed?"

"A few days at least. I will come tomorrow and attend her." She turned to Lydia. "Can you make sure she eats a good meal? She needs to gain her strength as it will speed her recovery. She is a little weak from the blood loss."

"Certainly."

Lord Danbye walked the midwife to the door and reached into his pocket for a coin. "For your troubles and also your silence, if you please?"

"You need not ask, my lord, but I thank you." She took the proffered coin and bid them good day.

~

THREE DAYS LATER, with daily care from the midwife, Cecily was back to her old self. Lydia was amazed at how quickly she had bounced back after such an ordeal. But she was young and now she was without the burden of impending motherhood and having to tell her parents, then life could go back to normal.

She was out of bed and dressed in a fresh set of clothes that Lydia had supplied. To look at her, one would think nothing had happened, and Lydia was glad for it. It had been an awful ordeal, but she hoped that Cecily would now be the wiser for it.

"Has Lord Danbye informed my parents that I am here yet?" Cecily asked her.

"Yes, he sent a message this morning. What tale are you going to tell them?"

"I think I am going to say that I fell in love with a man, although I will not mention who, and that I ran away to be with him but then changed my mind." She pulled a face. "Does that sound feasible? I mean, it is partly the truth."

"It is as good a truth as any. How do you think they will react?"

"I expect Papa will box my ears and Mama will take to her bed with smelling salts, but at least this truth will be better than the whole truth. I expect Papa will also interrogate me as to the name of the man so he can box his ears as well." She gave a mirthless laugh. "But I will not tell. John Russell is in my past and I will not think about him ever again." She looked down at her stomach. "And as for what happened, it is God's will."

Lydia's face grew sad, "I am sorry for your loss, Cecily but—"

"Say no more, Lydia. You have been a dear friend, as has Lord Danbye. Without you two, my life would now be in ruins. The outcome is for the best. Yes, I feel a loss, but it has made me realise how careful I must be." Her brow furrowed and her look became determined. "And also how I cannot trust men to do the right thing. I was too naive but not anymore."

"I am glad for you. You seem stronger." She hugged her before asking, "Will you return to court?"

"I would like to. I did enjoy it there. I just hope Queen Catherine will have me back." She sat down on a chair and nervously plucked at the folds in her skirt, clearly worried.

Lydia sought to calm her. "I honestly have no idea, Cecily. But we know her to be of a charitable nature and we also know that she likes you. So refrain from any doubt for now. Only time will tell."

Cecily smiled warmly at Lydia. "Your words bring me comfort and I thank you for it."

Lydia smiled in return and thought back to only a few months ago when the prospect of spending time with Cecily had been so abhorrent. How things had changed.

QUEEN CATHERINE DID INDEED ACCEPT CECILY BACK as a lady-in-waiting, although she gave her a good talking to about the merits of being virtuous and keeping men at bay. Her parents had also done the same. Cecily quietly accepted her fate and resumed her duties. John Russell was no longer in the employ of the court. Lord Danbye had made certain of it. A few harsh words in his ear and he had decided that moving away was in everyone's interests. Especially his own.

So life returned to normal at Seven Oaks. The long, heady summer evenings found Lydia either walking the surrounding fields filled with the scent of wildflowers or in the arms of her attentive husband. She had never been so happy or content.

One evening, lying with her head on her husband's lap at the base of a huge oak tree, Lydia stared up at him and realized how lucky she was. He was dominant but fair, and that was why she loved him so much. There was a quiet strength about him that made her feel safe, even if he did spank her a bit too often for her liking. But then, perhaps she needed someone to take her in hand occasionally.

She smiled up at him, her eyes soft. "Do you love me, my lord?"

He looked down at her lovingly. "You know I do, dearest Lydia."

"Even when I am naughty?"

"Especially when you are naughty." He grinned, showing his even white teeth, "For then, I get to chastise that naughty bottom of yours."

Lydia giggled. "My bottom is not naughty."

"I beg to differ. In fact, perhaps I should have another look now."

Lydia immediately squealed and jumped up, quickly running towards the house, her gay laughter filling the air and Lord Danbye's deep empty threats following straight after.

Percy stopped in his tracks and listened to their merriment, his own face breaking out in a smile. Seven Oaks was a grand house, but now, with the love that these two people shared, it was magnificent, and when the time came to hear the pitter patter of tiny feet, he hoped he would still be there to hear them.

For a love so strong was a rare thing indeed.

MARYSE DAWSON

Maryse Dawson was born in England but now lives in western France with her family. When she's not writing, she spends her time visiting the beaches and surrounding countryside.

She has always enjoyed reading romances and loves history, so began writing a few years ago to include domestic discipline in her stories.

You can find Maryse on Facebook at:
https://www.facebook.com/maryse.dawson.5

Don't miss these exciting titles by Maryse Dawson and Blushing Books:

Loving Lydia
Lost Love
A Kingdom Divided
Dark Secrets, An Anthology
A Knight to Remember
The General's Discipline
Mischief by Moonlight
Summer Scorchers
Royal Reward
Victorian Vixen
Protecting Aleida
A Pirate's Temptress

*Knights of Normandy series*

Renaud, Book One
Arthur, Book Two
Gerard, Book Three

*A Pirate's Treasure Series*
A Pirate's Treasure
A Pirate's Stowaway
The Captain's Lady

*The Beauty Series*
Innocent Beauty, Book One
Seductive Beauty, Book Two

*Moorland Maidens Series*
Rhona, Book One
Heather, Book Two
Alana, Book Three

*Anthologies*
Feisty Fables
Brat Tales Book One
Brat Tales Book Two
Beloved Brats
Devious Maidens
Romantic Tales
Lords & Ladies
Historical Heroes

# BLUSHING BOOKS

Blushing Books is the oldest eBook publisher on the web. We've been running websites that publish steamy romance and erotica since 1999, and we have been selling eBooks since 2003. We have free and promotional offerings that change weekly, so please do visit us at http://www.blushingbooks.com/free.

# BLUSHING BOOKS NEWSLETTER

Please join the Blushing Books newsletter
to receive updates & special promotional offers.
You can also join by using your mobile phone:
Just text BLUSHING to 22828.

Every month, one new sign up via text messaging will receive a
$25.00 Amazon gift card, so sign up today!